His Haunted Heart

Editing: Todd Barselow
Cover Design: Lila Felix
Photo: Shutterstock / Photographer: Roman Seliutin
Photographer: Swamp Scene/ Carlos Nunez

1. Young Adult Romance 2. Historical 3. Southern Gothic Romance 4. Paranormal-Ghost

Prologue

Pain was the closest I'd ever gotten to love.

The murky water at my feet frightened me. It wasn't the water itself, but what lay beneath, hiding, waiting to strike. But today, it was my only friend. At school, I'd made the most fatal of mistakes and here, by the edge of the pond that no one fished at any more, I waited for fate to catch up with me in the forms of my sisters with their jealous rage.

A bubble burst on the surface of the water and I jumped at the unwelcome noise. Fear had a deep grip in my gut and every noise sounded like death at my door.

Everyone had their breaking point. I was no exception. The chastising laughter of the other kids echoed in my thoughts. They'd formed a circle around me, pointing at my untruthful indiscretion.

"She sneaks out at night and earns her keep with the mayor."

The mayor part wasn't a stretch. It was well-known that since the mayor's wife died his visits to the Plots had become more and more frequent.

At the age of eighteen, I could, legally, work at the Plots. But I was no whore.

"They say her pretty face brings in bags and bags of money."

Another gulp of water was taken in by the pond, startling me. Most were terrified to visit this place. Sable, a girl of my age, had drowned herself in this pond years before. At least, that was the gossip. Her body was never recovered. No one cared enough to swim the depths for it. Two schools of thought surrounded her young suicide. The first was that it wasn't suicide at all. The second was that her father tormented her, making her quit school at an early age to work and beat her when she didn't make enough money. Unable to stand her life any longer, she put stones in the pockets of her dress and tied blocks to her own legs and drug herself to this liquid pit to meet her maker.

I could've understood the latter.

Most think of suicide as a selfish way to end one's life. They think of the tears shed and the guilt left to the families of the deceased. But I thought it was a gift. If she was a burden to the people around her, like I was, then maybe my early departure from this life would be a weight lifted. My parents would have one less mouth to feed; one less daughter to worry about marrying off; one less body to keep warm. And my sisters, well, their load would be lifted the greatest amount.

My sisters hated me. Adele and Elaine used picking on me as their full-time hobby. In my eyes, we each had our own distinct attributes. Adele was an excellent cook. Elaine could embroider so well that even the finest ladies in the town commissioned her work. Both were slim and beautiful in their own rights.

Somewhere along the line it had been decided that I was the prettiest. My figure was unlike those of my siblings. Where they were slim and gangly, I was a little curvier, though my underweight state hid most of that. My mother and sisters made the claim that I had no need of skills, like cooking or sewing, that my looks alone would afford me anything I wanted in life.

I tried to ignore it for the most part.

But that day, as the insults made me bleed, I caught the look on Geoffrey's face. He was embarrassed of being seen with me, maybe even more embarrassed than I was at being called a harlot.

They could hurt me all they wanted to, but Geoffrey was a good man. So I'd taken the opportunity, just that once, to take up for myself.

The fury on my sisters' faces was priceless. Until I realized that it would indeed cost me a dear price.

The winds through the Louisiana bayou cypress trees woke me from my dream state and reminded me with a chill what awaited me. Adele and Elaine were not ones to stand by and take what was doled out to them, no matter how much they deserved it. They were revenge-minded women and would seek it—aggressively.

"I may join you this night, Sable;" I whispered to the spirit trapped in the water below.

The sun setting in the distance forced me to stand up and take a deep breath, knowing my fate could be served hot or cold. It was that unknown that terrified me the most.

I took my time walking back to our home. From the outside, it was a normal home life personified. The shutters were perfectly in place, the door clean and steps swept. The best cleaning my mother did was that stoop. She kept the thing perfect. She did more sweeping at the front door than she ever did inside our home, the gossip and tearing down of her townsmen taking up the majority of her time.

Ever so gently, I turned the knob and it betrayed me at once, letting its owner know that I was home.

"There you are! Where have you been?" my father's boom barreled into me before the door had closed behind.

"I took a walk after school."

"Your sisters have been worried sick."

A guffaw broke from my lips before I could conceal it. They were worried that I'd offed myself before they could lay into me.

"I thought they'd be at the dance."

"And why didn't you go? They will be married with babes before you even begin to be courted. We can't support you forever you know."

"Yes, Father, I know. I will get to my chores now."

"You'd better. And you're too late for supper; you'll have to wait until tomorrow to eat."

Whatever grave crime I'd committed by being born, its punishment was meted out daily. Not in the form of beatings or other physical chastisements — it simply caused my parents to feel nothing for me.

I didn't know which was worse, hate or nonchalance.

After feeding the chickens and pigs, I washed up and went to bed in my nearly see-through hand-me-down gown. My stomach churned against itself, causing noises so loud, I was afraid I'd wake my parents and those wretched sisters of mine. Thinking I could sneak downstairs and steal a bit of bread, I tip-toed down one by one, purposefully avoiding the one that made a squeak. In the dark and in my half-sleep, I'd avoided the wrong one and stepped right on the offending stair, causing it to yelp in despair.

I froze, awaiting the oncoming blast of voices, but it never came.

Into the kitchen I crept and found the heel of a loaf of bread and stuffed it into my mouth before I was caught. They must've thought my so-called beauty could be used in exchange for food, as well, since I often was only given scraps or scrapings from the others' plates.

I didn't ask why — I just accepted my life for what it was and hoped that one day it would be a distant memory.

"And what do you think you're doing?" a boisterous slithered to my ear and caused me to jump.

"I was starving. It's just a piece of bread." I knew Adele's shrill voice like I knew my own palm.

"Who said you could have it?"

I turned to face her. "No one. This is my home too."

Elaine stepped into the scant moonlight filtering through the window. "She's gotten mouthy as of late. Perhaps she needs a bit of retraining."

They acted as if I was a disobedient horse.

"I was just defending myself," I said back with a pointed finger. I knew without a signal that our conversation had evolved into a confrontation about what had happened earlier at school.

"Again, who gave you permission?"

"I'm going to bed."

Adele and Elaine stepped together, looking like a pair of conjoined twins in the dark, one body and two heads, blocking my path.

"It's that pretty face that makes her so bold." Elaine said with a voice so dainty and a smile so vile.

"If something were to happen to that face, I bet she'd come down from her tower."

All of the sudden my sisters were poetic.

"Let me pass."

"You know, Father sharpened his knives today."

A tingling spider webbed down my face and neck while fear burrowed into the pit of my stomach. It had to be in jest. It had to be. "Be serious. That's a crime. You'd go to prison."

Adele shrugged. "Not if we kill you first. I'm sure the alligators would have a meal of you, no matter how measly it might be."

I tried to push through, but their chain was strong. "Hold her down, Elaine."

Elaine was the pudgiest of the three of us. Still, a tiny sliver of me thought this was all part of an elaborative scare tactic.

"Don't be stupid."

At that point, I was so nervous that stupid came out as *schtoopid* and they both laughed.

Before I knew what was happening, Elaine had knocked my feet out from under me and I was on my back, on the filthy floor where the rats played, with Elaine's robust rear end sitting on my stomach.

"Just along the side. We don't want her having an excuse for not working."

I heard the 'shing' of a knife being drawn from its sheath and it fueled me, giving me a rush, enough to release me from Elaine so I could run.

I only made it about five feet before she tackled me again, this time using all of her weight to push me against a wall near the staircase. Her hands fisted my hair, keeping me in place.

I struggled, trying to squirm my way out of her grip, but I was stuck. Her hip nailed me in place and I was useless against her hold on my roots.

This was it. I was going to die over a piece of bread.

Adele, somehow, lodged her arm across the front of my neck and pressed against my throat.

"Just wait until she passes out. It will be easier."

It sickened me even more that there was pre-meditation in their movements.

His
Haunted
Heart

I continued to fight as much as I could, but the edges of my vision began to blur and darken. Just before I faded out of consciousness, a singeing burn drew a line down the side of my once pretty, pretty face.

Chapter One

The last button on my sweater was cracked in half, but maintained its threads enough to complete the task it was knitted for. Neither blush-colored silk nor the pearls of a queen would help my plight unless they were fashioned into a mask that covered my face.

The last of the suitors would be at our door soon, and I would be expected to impress him with wit and intelligence since those were the only assets I had. It was embarrassing to say the least.

I had been pretty once, but that was all gone now.

My mother preached to me that marriages were about two complimentary personalities working together. Technically, she preached it to the fireplace, but I picked up the knowledge nonetheless. Yet, she constantly barraged me with speeches about how to sound smarter. I really shouldn't have taken advice from a woman whose response to being asked for a second helping of potatoes was to chuck the nearest water vessel at my father's head.

A suitor who chose me for my brain was problematic, according to my mother, in that it meant I would be marrying an imbecile.

My sister Adele married the clichéd rich, yet stupid man, who was brutish and carried around a lard vat of a belly. He picked his nose while no one was looking and grabbed my sister's backside when she went upstairs.

Elaine, my younger sister, married a smart man, but rail thin and, in her words, had a rail thin—well, other parts as well. It didn't seem to deter their public showings of affection or her getting pregnant on her wedding night.

At least she knew what to do on a wedding night.

I wouldn't even know what to expect after sputtering out vows that I was sure I wouldn't mean. We weren't allowed books on the subject or anything near the subject. And though I was sure my mother would oblige my concern, the last person I wanted to ask was her.

A knock at my bedroom door startled me and caused my heart to double-time in my chest. I knew she would be coming for this inevitable talk. This was my last chance. I had no long line of suitors breaking down the door, vying for my affections. I had a cold-tempered father and a mother who hated the very air I breathed, and together they wanted their eldest daughter out—which meant I would have to endure one last speech about answering questions properly and maintaining a humble attitude.

I had nothing but humility left. Humility was all I could afford.

The corn cake and stray piece of bacon fat from breakfast somersaulted in my stomach as I heard a second knock, this one at the front door of our home. The door was so tumbledown that for every rap of knuckles, it slammed back in place with a knock of its own. When I was a girl, the noise scared me, made me think that someone was coming into my room. My mother told tales of my sleepwalking, claiming to be following a playmate.

Pulling a bit of bone-straight raven hair over my face to cover some of the blasphemous scar, I looked down below and appraised the gentleman from my bedroom window, ignoring the knock at my own door. Though it was raining, I could see most of him through the curtain of drops. He was tall, even without the status-quo hat. His pants were ragged at the edges and in great need of a hem. Even the ends were a darker shade thanks to the sopped up water. Waiting for the door to be answered, he looked up. I gasped and ducked out of sight. He needed not see me before he absolutely had to. Even if we were married, he would probably whole-heartedly agree to look at me as little as possible.

The overheard gossip of my sisters assured me that any marital duties would be handled in the dark, either way which contradicted their entire premise for ruining my pretty face. Then again, their claim to grabbing their perfect husbands was by the brow of their looks.

My gaze was redirected across the way to a tiny girl standing at the cusp of the town, just in my line of sight. She was three or four years old at the most. She stared directly at me, her white dress, old-fashioned for the early nineteenth century, billowing in the bayou breeze. The Louisiana swamps on the edge of the street seemed to weep with the rain, tired of being overcrowded. But not the girl. The rain didn't faze her in the least. In fact, her dress was untouched by any wetness at all. It didn't droop or cling to her form.

Movement caught my eye. Looking back to the street below, the man was now gone, having come into the house. Panic gripped my insides and shook them for effect. Having to face another condescending suitor was last on my personal list of things to do today.

I chanced one more look at the girl, but she was gone. Her mother had probably caught up with her, dragging her out of the rain.

My mother came in, unwelcomed, and started in right away. "Delilah, he's here. Heavens above, is that what you're wearing? You look like a thundercloud come down to visit."

Her face was made of the thunderclouds, so if anyone would know the look, it was her.

Shuffling my worn boots, I looked down and appraised my garb. "It's the best I have besides my plum dress. He certainly won't choose me for my looks. It doesn't matter, anyway."

"It matters. Trust me, it matters." She approached me and I stepped back out of habit, though my mother had never physically struck me. "If this man offers you his hand in marriage, you must accept. Let's be honest. There weren't many to begin with and there won't be another one after this. We can't be throwing food down another gullet."

Though her case for me getting married was laughable, I didn't dare speak against her. My sisters both came over for breakfast and sometimes tea, nearly every day—even though their houses were bountifully stored with any food they wanted.

Of course, they were beautiful and refined.

Beauty granted women anything in this world.

Which is why I had nothing.

"I'm sorry, Mother. If he makes an offer, I will go—no matter what. You needn't worry."

I'd apologized for my parents having to feed me. Then again, I apologized for everything — just in case.

My words and tone addressed her as though she were a mother who actually cared whether or not I was wedded to a troll or an insolent murderer. As long as she no longer had to see me and my wretched face at the table, everything would be well.

I did what I could to help them. Working for three different households, doing all their laundry, brought in a decent amount of money, but my father demanded the lot of it, claiming that it didn't even equal how much I ate. I handed it all over without complaint.

I was used to it.

It wasn't a revelation, the disdain of my father. From the time I was born, he'd been adamant about my air of vanity and haughtiness. He claimed that he would break me of it one way or the other.

The notion was silly, that I attained any measure of vanity.

I wasn't vain. I knew that I was pretty — just like the other girls. I knew I was thin — mostly because I was only given scraps to eat, like the family pet. And I knew I was smart because I had good marks in school.

Vanity wasn't my friend and I took no comfort in her. Even if I had, she granted me no favor.

My face was ripped open—a fatality of my own sisters' war on vanity, as if the society we lived in didn't hold enough protestable sins.

Still, an ember of hope lay lit in my chest, telling me that there was someone who could still love me.

It probably wasn't the man downstairs.

"Good. Now get yourself down there. Let's not keep him waiting. We've got enough of an apology coming down the stairs without adding to it," she added, flicking my cracked button with a grimace. I allowed myself one last look to the rain before succumbing to her pull. The rain had always calmed me and the rumble of the thunder reminded me that I was alive.

With her hand pinching my elbow, she shuffled me down the stairs; the bass of two male voices going back and forth could be heard over the crackle of the fire. A discussion was being had about whether or not the man in question could properly provide for a girl of my stature. My father might as well have asked him if he could afford to feed the heifer. The banter was so curt and strained, it sounded almost rehearsed.

"She wouldn't need for a thing—that I can guarantee you."

A grunt was my father's only response. That and the squeak of his rocking chair were the only noises in the room. Maybe I could sneak in and just serve as a silent audience to this auction for their gnarly beast of a daughter.

The last stair creaked and announced our arrival. It was the same creak that usually made the mice shuffle about, scampering back to their homes and announced to everyone the one time I'd snuck downstairs to grab a piece of bread to subdue my gurgling stomach.

"That's *her*."

The vision of my face was so grotesque that even my own father thought I didn't warrant a name.

"Your name?" The tall gentleman took a step forward, his face coming into the light of the fire. A strong-looking jaw worked back and forth as I stuttered out my name and something akin to 'pleased to meet you'. He was easily five inches taller than me and as he got closer, his shadow made an umbrella over mine. I shrunk back, frightened and intrigued at the sight of him. His eyes matched the color of the smoke that billowed in every chimney in the village. They bore into me as the hint of a sideways smile began, but never took shape. Surely, this whole scenario was in jest. A man of his degree of handsome would never stoop to a betrothal with me. It must've been one of my sisters' idea of a sick bit of comedy.

"Delilah. A lovely name. Can you cook?"

A dastardly question if there ever was one. My mouth opened, but my father interjected before my tongue could conjure a proper response. The man's stare was still locked with mine and I could hardly work up a thought, much less a word. "She can cook, clean, wash the clothes and we are confident all your other needs will be met."

My belly soured hearing my father speak of me as though I was a sow in heat. It wasn't the first time my father had been unabashedly lewd and revolting when boasting of my wifely skills. Bile rose in my throat and by instinct I turned away from the whole scenario. The gentleman, who stood stoic, would soon be disappointed if he believed one word my father said.

"Excellent. If Delilah would have me, we would be married in the morning."

My knees buckled. I barely caught myself on the wobbly bannister of the stairs behind me before I slumped onto the filthy floor. Father had barely taken three puffs of his cigar and a proposal was made. What nonsensical man does that?

My father smiled, revealing teeth dotted with tobacco pith. "She'll have you. Would you like to eat with us tonight?"

I didn't see the point in prepping me for instant acceptance of any proposal if they were just going to answer for me.

"I'd be honored. Thank you."

At once, my mother scuttled into the kitchen, with a firm grip on my skirt, dragging me along. My head was swimming with prospects and at that point, none of them were good.

Her dusky apron was tied around her waist as she planned with a finger pointed at me.

"We'll make chicken and roasted vegetables. That's sure to warm his belly and keep him satisfied."

With jerky movements, I wrenched the carrots, turnips, and potatoes from their bins. God forbid my parents actually offer me a congratulations or at least something close to it. A relief warmed my chest as I chopped up the meal's accompanying vegetables. This was it. Answering a couple of questions and cooking a meal was the price of my freedom. I sent up a silent prayer that I wasn't trading the devilish duo for Beelzebub himself.

My intelligence wasn't needed after all, which frightened me more than it should've.

Maybe all that was expected of me would be obedience.

Obedience I could handle.

Just as it came, the relief faded and was replaced by skepticism—a gnawing that curled my insides and made me pop my head into the living room more than once to verify the truth of his presence. He'd seen my face, I knew that. Yet, not a word was said about it and no mention of anything else was muttered.

Something beneath the surface must be wrong with this man.

While I allowed doubting thoughts to meander through my mind, I watched my mother prep the chicken to be roasted. She'd never allowed me into the kitchen and so, the boasting of my cooking skills was dishonest at best.

I hoped there was a slim possibility of me learning the craft of chicken roasting in one afternoon. That way, Mr. 'Can you cook?' wouldn't go hungry and throw me to the street. We'd have chicken every night, but neither of us would starve.

"Start the coffee and the biscuits. Don't just stand there like a twit."

"I don't know how to make biscuits." She turned around, looking shocked and then recognized the accusation in my squint. It was her fault she'd never taught me to cook. She was always afraid that I'd excel at something — anything — and maybe outshine the other three women in the house. "Yes, well, I'll make them. Just start the coffee and get Gran's good tablecloth from the cabinet."

There was no use getting the good stuff out now. He'd probably already seen the decrepit floors and the layer of aged soot around the fireplace. It wasn't as if he thought he was dining with royalty. I shrugged and retrieved the tablecloth after putting the kettle on to boil. A stray rag was used to swipe the crumbs from the table and into my hand. There was no use in putting a cloth on top of crumbs, it would be like throwing a curtain over the pebbles on the beach.

I'd never seen the beach, but I'd read about it.

An hour later, everything was ready and the table was set. Halfway through the meal, a question rose in my mind and in my critical situation, I didn't know whether or not to broach the subject or keep my mouth shut until the vows were exchanged. My father seemed to acknowledge the oncoming question and pointed his knife in my direction, effectively slicing the question from my tongue before it had a chance to coalesce.

I glanced at the stranger, now my betrothed, to see if he could detect the family strife beneath the clanking of forks and knives. What I didn't expect, when my eyes met his, was the concern written on his pristine, un-marred face.

"You don't eat much," he regarded with a nod to my plate.

"Usually she gorges like a cow," my mother snapped, her cheeks puffed full of her own ball of cud. When she spoke, her eyes never left her plate, concerned that some of her chicken would vanish if she didn't offer it constant worship.

"Yet, you remain a slip of a thing. Strange." He spoke directly to me, ignoring the false jab.

Pooching my lips together, I defied the rising smile. Already he could see right through my mother's antics. Maybe he wasn't as stupid as I'd assumed.

There must've been some secret deformity if he'd chosen me.

The rest of the meal went off without a hitch and before I knew it I was already feeling as if I'd left this place yet was no closer to knowing where I was going or who I was going with.

I only owned three skirts, three shirts with ragged corsets and various other garments including two sweaters, more like glorified rags—and one dress left behind by Adele. I didn't even own a coat and my only pair of shoes was a worn-thin pair of lace up boots that had been thrown to the garbage bin by a woman I washed clothes for.

"You've got everything?" My mother barged into my room at the break of day, and seemed to have a genuine concern though I could see right through it. I'd been up since dawn, staring out the window, letting the promise and curse of my future flit through my mind.

I nodded to my suitcase. "It's all in here."

During the night, I'd wondered if I would be provided a wedding dress like the other girls, or maybe even just a clean, patch-free dress. It was less of a question and more of an unrequited hope. None of those things ever came. When the sun broke through my window, giving up on the prospect, I dressed in my plum-colored dress with a black fitted coat on top, my best, and ruined the little beauty the ensemble contained coupling it with my failing boots. I'd tangled my hair into a loose braid so that it hung over my left shoulder, masking the part of me he'd regret being wed to.

The man had already seen my face, this outfit would probably serve as a welcomed distraction as it showed a great deal of the upper swell of my breasts. Even my threadbare jacket couldn't contain them.

"You can't take your blankets and things. Those will be needed for the boarders."

Less than twelve hours and my parents had already arranged to have my absence serve as a steady income. It was no surprise. People were always in and out of town and most families had at least one room that served as extra income. It was a small town, more like a village and newcomers didn't stay long, either pushed out or turned off.

"That's fine, Mother. I'm sure they've got blankets."

"Well, you best get to the church. Do everything he asks, Delilah. You don't want to be sent to the Plots."

My mother's best threat, other than her stringing backhand, was that I'd be destined to go to the Plots.

The Plots were the whore houses on the outskirts of our village and if you were thrown out of your home, other than the poverty stricken lifestyle of the laundry washers and maids, prostitution was the profession that chose you. Either that or a slow death due to starvation.

Though sometimes I wondered how much worse selling yourself could be in comparison to being hated by your own family.

From her clipped tone and the finality in her words, I assumed they wouldn't be present at my wedding. Though unrelished tears stung the corners of my eyes at the thought, I knew it was better this way. There were no feelings between us other than obligation and I was no longer their responsibility. Even so, remorse for a better set of parents washed through me, wishing they were at least interested in seeing me married.

With a cold nod, I grabbed my suitcase—which was, if possible, more worn than my boots and made my way downstairs. My father was at work, so no goodbye was necessary. Still, I turned one last time and took in everything I wouldn't miss—the rat infested cupboards, the dingy rugs, and the scratch on the wall where the knife had sliced after it was done with my face and my back.

A slammed door behind me was my official goodbye.

The walk through town was almost embarrassing. By now, word of my marriage to-be had gotten around. Waiting until my age of twenty-three was unheard of in this place. Women in their fine attire whispered to each other in couples. Owners of stores walked outside and crossed their arms over their chests.

I hung my head low and kept my eyes on the ground as the bells of the chapel beckoned me to the call. There was no point in looking around anymore. The buildings and windows of the town were wrapped in a film of amber dust that seemed to reproduce from thin air. It was as though the Lord had drawn in a great breath and instead of releasing the blowing wind, blew a blast of rusty dust everywhere. It clung to my lungs and provided a canvas for the children in the street to draw in.

Finally, I reached the church. A blast of warm air washed over my face when I opened the chapel doors. Our town chapel was as dirty as the rest of the town and in terms of the condition of souls, maybe even filthier. The air felt good on my chapped cheeks and on the frigid tips of my ears. The pews were empty and the smell of beeswax burning candles filled my nose.

"You made it Delilah." Surprise blanketed his face as though I was the one in this equation who was the unknown.

The man liked to say my name, and I couldn't deny the buzzing warmth in my belly when he did. No one had ever said my name with such emotion behind it. But in less than a day, how could any emotion back up my name on his tongue? "Where are your parents?"

"They're not coming. I'm sorry..." I gestured toward my dress while he strode toward me down the middle aisle. There was a purpose in his steps and a stir in his eyes that I did not recognize.

"You look beautiful. All this black hair..." He pulled at the ends of my braid and cleared his throat. "Let's get this over with."

At least the consensus on this marriage was unanimous — everyone wanted the deed done in a rush.

A flash of emotion crossed his features as he spoke of my hair, but when I'd gasped, it all whooshed out of the room taking his smoky gaze with it. I thanked the Lord for that moment of clarity. I understood what I was up against. Hot and cold was certainly better than raging hate. I nodded and answered, "Yes, please."

The local Constable and his wife stood as witnesses while the priest read his stiff vows for us to repeat, preferably with some emotion. Neither I, nor my fiancé, were able to summon such things. No blame for it would be put on my betrothed's hands, since anyone in their right mind couldn't be all that much in adoration at the thought of pledging their life to be spent with a roughed up creature like me.

I tugged at my dress, uncomfortable standing opposite this finely dressed man, holding my hands, making promises neither he nor I knew whether or not we could keep. Even the Constable's wife seemed enamored with him. Her eyes flicked to his form more than once during the ceremony.

"Porter Quentin Jeansonne do you take Delilah Catherine Sharp to be your lawful wedded wife?"

Porter. His name was Porter. The first thing I'd learned about my new husband was his name.

No matter what his name was, he was my savior.

He was also a good bit older than me. His date of birth was scribbled on the certificate—he was twenty-seven to my twenty.

He must've been as desperate to marry as my parents were to get rid of me.

The rest of the ceremony was more of the same icy procedure, signing forms and curt nods of the head.

It was when the priest said, 'Go, enjoy your marriage and be fruitful' that the weight of what had occurred that morning settled like a brick in the pit of my stomach.

There would be expectations and the fear of them gurgled into my throat and down to my toes, anchoring in place.

Porter must've seen the damned things grow into concrete blocks because he took my hand and with a swift pull, bid me follow him.

On our way to the exit, I bent to retrieve my suitcase but I was beat to it by my new husband. "Let me."

He offered me his arm. I'd never been offered the arm of a gentleman in my life. Even in my younger days, the rumors my sisters spread about me were so foul that no one dared come into my presence, much less offer me a kindness.

My first kiss had been a taken one behind the school building—he must've been dared.

No one in their right mind would kiss someone like me.

"Thank you, Sir." No correction was made, in my address, so I assumed that was how he preferred me answer him. He nodded once then gestured toward a black horse with cinnamon tipped ears that seemed just as happy to have me on him as I was at the prospect of riding the beast. "We are to ride that?"

A black gloved hand covered his mouth and a laugh, but the slight crinkle in the corner of his eyes could not be covered. He was laughing at me.

"He is a gentle one. Don't be afraid. You didn't strike me as a female who is easily frightened and you still don't."

"Is that why you chose me?"

My question caused him to grow rigid in gait and look around the town as if to check if anyone was listening. They all were. Nothing could be done in our town without it being a community affair. Hunching my shoulders in regret, I punished myself for my unwarranted words by biting into my bottom lip as hard as I could. The metallic taste told me I'd done well.

"We will talk later."

My suitcase was hoisted onto the side of the saddle and fastened in place with a rope. Porter — I would call him that in my mind if nothing else — with one foot in a stirrup, mounted the monster and with an outstretched hand, asked me to follow his lead. I did so without an ounce of grace, and before I could settle myself in, we were in a full gallop, to where, I had no idea.

Chapter Two

The entire way home, time after time, I checked if she was still behind me, her willowy body barely hanging on. I feared the wind would sweep her away from me. We crossed the last bridge before the final road that led to my home and I patted the outside of my new bride's thigh, checking once more that she was still with me.

"I'm here," she assured me with her small voice. It was the first time she'd spoken on the journey. I'd expected questions and observations about every little thing since I lived on the outskirts of The Rogue and within the denser, more darkened part of the swamps—places most people never went. I'd assumed she had never visited these parts, so her silence concerned me.

I filled the time with recurring visions of her home and the first time I'd seen her. The issues her parents thought themselves clever in hiding, I'd seen clear as day. Their rotund bellies compared to her sunken cheeks spoke volumes.

The compounded soot along the edges of their tired fireplace told a story of a matriarch that took no pride in her home, yet claimed she'd taught her daughter how to be a good wife. The only lessons Delilah had been taught were fear and self-loathing. The fact was apparent in the way she held herself, her hesitance to look me in the eyes, and mostly in the reluctance I felt in the way she refused to hold me properly as we rode.

There were crimes committed against the small creature at my back that I may never be able to undo.

She'd called me Sir. I would correct her later, away from the intruding eyes of the townsfolk.

It would be better for her that way, for the townspeople to perceive our marriage as a chaste decision made by two people, both past the normal marrying age — me more so than her. I wondered if I should keep it from her, the pretensions of our relationship.

I couldn't imagine a right place or time for that conversation, but if she asked, I would be obliged to tell her the truth.

Meandering thoughts flitted through my mind, filling the space between the bridge and the estate.

Finally, we were home and I didn't know who was more nervous, me or Delilah.

Judging by her wringing fingers, I guessed it was her.

My home, a darkened shadow of a mansion, came more and more into focus as I turned onto the gravel road. The sun was pitched in the clouds, welcoming us, providing a light that burst through the tiny spaces between clumps of Spanish moss and provided wind chimes made of rays that hung from the branches. As we drew closer, the curtains in several windows of the house moved with their masters' fingers, spying on the gift I'd brought home.

A gasp reminded me that I hadn't said a word to her, matching her silence to me. "This is Jeansonne Manor. This is our home."

Wiry fingers tightened on my shirt where it was tucked into my trousers. She was frightened. I didn't blame her. There was a looming air about my childhood home that worked to our advantage, keeping the nosey away and holding its tenants tight. The past cast its darkness over our home a long time ago and burrowed the goodness down under its wings for none to find—none except those who sought it.

"It's so beautiful," Delilah murmured against my back. The warmth of her whisper permeated my jacket and shivered down my spine. I hadn't expected this initial reaction to her presence. I didn't know what I expected.

I barely remembered to answer her.

"I'm glad you think so."

"There are other people." Her statement was intonated like a question and I thought I heard relief in her voice.

"Yes, my mother is here, but she will move into the guest house today or tomorrow. There is a chef, a maid, and a stable boy."

A few minutes passed and I stopped Benjamin, my horse, with a slow pull of the reins. I jumped off of the horse and before I could offer assistance, Delilah had hopped down and was stretching from side to side. Her eyebrows were bunched at the bridge of her nose.

"Are you in pain?" I stepped toward her while speaking.

"It was a long ride. I'm not used to riding a horse."

"You can stretch your legs while I give you a tour of the house—our house." She seemed to beam at the prospect and I took advantage of it, grabbing her cold, delicate hand in my own. There was an absence to my wife's hand. "Also, I have your ring upstairs in the bedroom, please remind me if I forget. It is too valuable to me to travel with, so I left it here."

She lifted her face to look me in the eyes. The spreading warmth in my chest made me feel like I'd been waiting my whole life to have her look at me. There, under the overcast of a knuckled oak tree, one of her eyes shown a tint lighter than the other.

The sun shifted above us. It was then that I really saw that glinting silver line down her face. She'd tried to cover it with her hair, but I knew it was there. It was almost perfect in its imperfection. As if it needed to be there to remind me that she was human and not ethereal. It brought her back down to Earth, but did nothing to detract from her angelic beauty.

"Who hurt you?" I whispered two of my fingers along the mark, hoping that my concern seeped through in my words. I was sure it didn't. I was known more for my callousness than my charm.

She shrunk back at my words, shifting her eyes to the ground, but didn't shy from my touch.

"Not yet." Her sweet breath touched my face as she covered my fingers with her hand, keeping me there.

"Everything in time. I understand. Come on. They've been waiting a long time for me to bring home a bride."

Her nose crinkled at my words, but she didn't pull away when I enfolded her hand into my arm. Delilah was devilish yet innocent in that dress that showed me just enough to fill my mind with temptation beyond anything I'd ever experienced. We approached the house and just before we reached the door, my mother Eliza, came out, her smile showing the excitement I'd tamed, barely.

My mother's guilt over what was once my almost-marriage to Marie nearly equaled mine. She shouldn't have to bear any of it. It was all my doing. I'd tried to love Marie—I had.

By the time I'd given up on the notion, she had too.

"Mother, this is Delilah. Delilah, this is my mother, Eliza."

My new bride bowed her head in respect. It was a formal gesture from The Rogue, but the tradition had been lost a long time ago.

"It's so very nice to meet you, Mrs. Jeansonne."

My mother waved her hand in disgust of such formality. "It will be Eliza, my new daughter. You are most welcome here. Come and have tea with me after Porter gives you the tour of the house. You're a flit of a thing, you must be hungry. But my goodness, you are a beauty."

Delilah ignored the compliment. "Only if you have something prepared. I ate plenty last night."

My mother looked astonished. The pleasantly plump woman was probably already working on her third meal of the day. "This is your home now, Delilah. Eat when you wish and eat your fill. Porter is an excellent businessman and we can afford to eat well as you can see." Mother patted her belly with pride. I gauged my new wife's response to my mother's announcement of my wealth, but if she was impressed or disgusted, no one would be able to tell.

"Thank you. I'd like to wash up a bit after the tour and then I will join you."

"Good. I'll put the kettle on. Porter, show the girl around her new home."

Delilah's hand had fisted the fabric of my jacket while I made her introduction. A touch of pride stung me, relieved that at the very least I could be someone for her to hold onto. Looking down on her, her head barely coming up to my chin, I noticed her marked shiver. Already I was making a poor showing as a husband.

"Mother," I called out before the over-exuberant woman got too far.

"Yes?"

"A change of plan. My wife is freezing and probably hungrier than she's letting on. I doubt she was given anything more than scraps at her home. I'm going to settle her in front of the fire in the main living room. Bring her food and tea there, please."

I saw the protest building in Delilah's eyes, but I put a swift stop to it by bending a bit and whispering in her ear. "Let me take care of my wife. I'm learning here, Mrs. Jeansonne. You wouldn't begrudge me that, would you?"

She shook her head no with a blaring blush and I chuckled. I'd thought she'd put up a fight. Her stomach was probably overriding the notion.

I led her through the hallway and into the main parlor. I placed her in my chair at the side of the fireplace and reached for a blanket, one that my mother had knitted along with most of the blankets in our home. As I draped it over her thin legs, I took inventory of her physical needs. She was in desperate need of another pair of boots. Her sweater was way too thin to ever protect her from the elements. I should've noticed that before bringing her home by horse, but nothing could be done to remedy that error. The mistake wouldn't be repeated. I wasn't used to looking after anyone other than myself. My mother and the other people in the house each managed their own way.

"This is too much." She rebelled and refused to look at me again, making a feeble attempt to get up. I nixed the motion with my hand on her knee.

"Consider it making up for lost time," I said, kneeling beside the chair and, tucking the blanket around her. "Are you warming up?"

"I am. Thank you, Sir."

"I am Porter to you. You are my wife, not my employee."

A slight bite of her lip and I was caught in her snare—a snare I doubted she even knew she'd set.

"I've got bread, cheese, fresh fried ham, and cake. It's not much, but it's a start."

I laughed at my mother's candor. The tray contained more food than Delilah had probably ever seen at one sitting. She'd have the poor girl stuffed to the brim in less than a week.

"We will leave you to rest a bit now, won't we Port?"

Hesitation stilled me. I didn't want to leave her yet. Fear trickled down into my gut, telling me that she would leave, no prospects or not, simply to get away from this place and the grunt she'd been made to marry. I supposed smothering her less than a day after we'd been married would equally cause her to flee, so I took my leave, but not without reluctance.

Instead of checking in on her, minute by minute, I went to the office, in the back of the house, and buried myself in paperwork. My business, unbeknownst to anyone in the town, was with people in the world outside The Rogue. There was no money to be made in the town. There were only so many butcher, bakers, and sin-house makers one population could handle.

I sat at my desk and though there was plenty to do, my thoughts drifted back to her.

I wasn't naïve. This was no regular marriage. Delilah wasn't swept off her feet by my undying love and persistent ploys to win her affections. Her father had been all but selling her on the streets of The Rogue. Initially, I'd felt sorry for whoever the chit was, but when I saw her face, it was no longer a case of charity, but a case of compulsion.

I had to know her.

I needed to know her.

Only a half an hour passed before I heard a voice. "Am I interrupting?"

Shocked at anyone in my office, I jumped, throwing papers every which way. She rushed into the office, apologizing and picking it all up before I could even recuperate from my start.

"It's fine. Leave them. No one ever comes into my office. You scared me."

Delilah's face paled past alabaster and crossed into downright ghostly. "I'm so sorry. I'll leave."

My hand snapped out, grabbing her wrist to stop her from fleeing. "I meant no one has ever come into my office. You are welcome wherever I am."

Half of a day and I'd turned into a sap.

"I finished with the meal and returned the tray to the kitchen. They wouldn't let me help clean — your mother and June. They said you were in the office."

"I owe you a tour, don't I?" Changing the conversation instantly calmed her. She sat back on her haunches and crossed her arms over her chest. The gesture was surely defensive. "You must need to unpack your things."

She glanced out of the window, acknowledging the passing of time. "I should do that before tonight."

A blush flourished across her cheeks and flooded her neck. My thoughts were in the same line of thought as her blush, but I knew, again, this was no ordinary marriage.

"I will show you the bedroom and maybe you'd enjoy a hot bath. My mother claims a hot bath can cure all ailments. There are some things I had brought in for you."

Her eyebrows bunched in confusion. "We just met last night."

"I'd spoken to your father last week, Delilah. It was merely a choice of asking for your hand in person. He insisted that I meet you before I'd decided anything."

The revelation didn't pain her as much as I'd anticipated. When I'd spoken the words, I thought for sure I'd erred again. At least she didn't know that I'd practically paid for her.

"Oh, I see. He's been trying to pawn me off on someone for years. I bet you feel like a sucker right now, don't you?"

"Actually, it feels like winning. Let me show you our bedroom."

Chapter Three

If Porter didn't stop saying the word 'bedroom' over and over in such a nonchalant manner, I would shrivel up and die right there on the floor of his office. I got up off my backside with his assistance and tripped my way up his mountain of stairs, mahogany, shined, without a creak to be heard.

There must've been a hundred rooms in the place. Porter didn't go into any of them. He stood in the doorway and explained who had once slept there or who had redecorated. Each bedroom boasted a unique color theme and for my own peace of mind, I would name them after those colors. I sighed, following his footsteps to the other side of the house, wondering how many more rooms I had to remember. For such a beautiful home, navigating it would be murder.

"This wing is our bedroom."

Tingling in my head alerted me. He must be lying. He thought he could trick the girl with the wicked scar.

"The entire wing is a bedroom?"

The audacity of this man, trying to fool me.

"Well, not the entire thing. There's a bathroom, a reading room, the bedroom, and both of our closets."

He reached for two brass knobs and turned them, pushing the double doors open and revealing his truth. My new bedroom was bigger than two of my old houses put together.

"Heavens above," I gasped.

"It was my parents' bedroom. My father spoiled my mother rotten. She hasn't slept in here since my father died years ago. Make yourself at home. There is running water, hot and cold here. No need to heat it over the fire."

I didn't know where to turn first. I'd heard murmurings of running water from the townsmen who did business in the other world. But to have access to it…

There was the other issue. I couldn't break my gaze from the bed. A four-poster bed from another era sat in the middle of the room. The carvings along the posters and headboard were vines and roses of every shape and size, complete with thorns. Dark teal velvet curtains were drawn at the sides and held there with a cord of gold rope.

Unable to help myself, I looked at Porter who seemed to be under as much duress as I was.

"Delilah," he said as he approached. I stood true. I refused to be afraid of this life like I was in the last.

"Porter."

"I don't expect anything from you tonight or any night until we are both willing. Don't mistake me, you are beautiful and I won't hide the fact that I want you. But I will wait until the feeling is mutual. Until then, I will be sleeping down the hall in the Grover bedroom."

"Green."

"Green?"

"Grover's room is green. I couldn't remember all the names, so I memorized them by color. Green sounded like Grover. It was easy to remember."

He chuckled and the sound shattered the anxiety I'd built up. "That's smart. I'll get some of my clothes for tomorrow and then be out of your way. Supper is in two hours."

"I'm sorry," I blurted. My back was turned to him but I spun around to see his face. I was nothing if not self-punishing. "I'm sure I'm not the wife you'd hoped for."

He stilled and for the second time in a day, I punished my lips for their outburst. From his previous doting, I half-expected a declaration on bended knee. Instead, he looked at me over his shoulder and clenched his fist. "You're everything I wanted and more."

Without another word, he gathered his things and left me, closing the door behind him.

After the longest, warmest bath I'd ever had, I waited for something to happen. The house was quiet below and around me. Dressed in a gray skirt that came down almost to my ankles and a pink empire-waist blouse, I grabbed a black sweater before descending the massive stairs. I felt disjointed from the entire day's events, as though they were happening to me in a dream and I was merely the audience. Slipping on my corrupted black boots reminded me that if, in fact, it was a dream then certainly I could imagine a better looking pair of shoes.

A gentle smile blossomed on my face thinking of my new husband. Certainly, I was standing on the edge of reality, just in the valley of the real Porter coming forth. No part of the scenario thus far made sense. Porter was wealthy, kind, and probably the most handsome man I'd ever seen. There had to be a flaw. No one so flawless would come searching much less settle for someone like me.

I steeled myself to enjoying the dream while it lasted.

I left the room and placed one foot on the top step when a figure at the bottom of the stairs appeared. My heart halted in my chest and my lungs arrested in surprise. It was the same child as I'd seen the day before. Her blonde hair and iridescent blue eyes were the same, yet this child was different.

Her dress was white again, in the same fashion with flared sleeves that reminded me of a portrait of Juliet as she wept over Romeo. Her baby-like chubby cheeks were now a little gaunter and her bare feet were now covered with simple ballet flats befitting her age. Though there was no draft and no open door, the fabric that clothed her waved in a phantom breeze, enhancing her empyrean appearance.

This child was clearly a bit older.

A chair behind the girl could be seen — through her body — and she spoke to me. Her mouth moved, coupled with a pained expression. The sorrow on her face was so palpable that I almost ran down to her and attempted to scoop her up, translucent or not.

Porter's mother, emerged from one of the living rooms and clapped with glee. "There you are! Supper will be ready soon. Are you okay?"

I pointed with a shaking hand to the girl, only to find that she wasn't there.

"What is it, child?"

The space was empty, bare of any sign of the girl.

"Nothing. I thought I saw something."

"What did you see?"

Eliza didn't seem half as shocked as I would've expected. I looked down at the plump woman now staring into the space previously occupied by the girl.

"What did I see?" I parroted back to her.

"Delilah, this is an old home, owned by many before my husband and me. Plus the way the sun peers through the windows casts shadow all over the place. I've gotten a scare more times than I could count."

In a roundabout way, she was trying to give clout to my sighting without expressing direct validity.

"I understand."

For the second time that day, she waved a hand in the air, dismissing me. "You've had a trying day. A wedding and a journey. You probably need a good meal and a decent night's sleep, that's all."

I'd never sat down to a decent meal followed by a peaceful night's sleep. If she claimed it would cure me, then perhaps I could've been well years ago. I made my way down the stairs and looked for Porter. A longing for the touch of my new husband caught me by surprise. I longed for the warmth and callous of his hands on mine. My hands fisted at my sides, wishing they were grasping his coat or his shirt instead of the air.

I felt a sense of safety with him — probably unfounded and naïve.

"Maybe you're right. A meal and some sleep will help." Following her to the dining room, I saw that Porter stood near the far end, hands clasped behind his back, staring out the window that faced a haze-covered pond which could only be seen by the light of the bayou moon. I must've taken longer in the bath than I'd thought. Then again, everything in this place, from the time the horse clomped its feet on the driveway, fell under the tint of a dusky disposition.

He'd changed clothes, now clad in a loose fitting cream-colored shirt and simple gray trousers. Eliza cleared her throat as we passed the threshold. Porter inhaled a quick breath and turned around, causing me to muffle my own gasp. He was different, relaxed and casual, with his hair tousled.

He almost looked carefree.

"Did you enjoy your bath?"

My chin bowed with embarrassment. "I did. Thank you. It was like swimming."

A chuckle broke free of both Porter and his mother. I hadn't meant the comment in jest, but apparently they found humor in it. I would've taken humor over hate any day.

"Sorry."

"Don't be sorry. It's been a while since we had a laugh around here. Porter is too serious for us all."

Porter shot his mother a look that I perceived as a silent signal that she'd revealed too much.

"Did you find your gifts?" he prompted after a few seconds of uncomfortable silence.

"I did. But, I can't accept them."

His posture grew rigid as I spoke. A sprig of dark brown hair fell from its place and wafted across his forehead, equally offended as Porter obviously was. Already I'd said something wrong in less than a day. It seemed I would never learn to keep my mouth shut.

"Why not?"

I flicked at the edges of my sweater. Some women might've jumped at the chance to have nice things and expensive clothing. I'd grown comfortable in my station in life and the things it afforded me. Dressing me up would be like having a hand-crafted door fitted to a shamble of a shack. The clothes I wore suited the look of me.

I stuttered out, "I'm not used to them. I can't just change who I am in a day and no amount of fine clothes will change what I look like. It's like trying to dress up a possum."

Another giggle erupted from Eliza as she attempted to quietly leave the conversation. "Port, I will retrieve the food from the kitchen while you clear this up." Clear this up was enunciated for some reason. I felt the welts of the incoming scolding before it had even begun.

She took her leave and as the door shut behind her, Porter approached me. My initial thought was that the glass that was this whole day had finally cracked. I'd cracked it wide open with my words. Would he strike me or use hurtful words—or both? I didn't know.

"Delilah." He breathed my name like a prayer and as his warm breath flowed over my face, so did a knowing that no harm would come to me. "Please don't say such things. This is such a small part of you." His thumb traced the path of the cut, this time starting at my chin and ending up at the top, near my temple.

"There's more," I confessed.

"Where?"

Didn't he know that he'd just asked the most intimate question of them all? I hefted out a heavy breath and stilled myself, silently building a wall to lean against. This was my husband now, not just a stranger though I'd known him less than a day. The least I could do was to look him in the eyes and give him the full truth of who I was—no matter how disgraceful.

"Along my back." Gazing into his eyes, searching for a response, he blinked several times. His hands blazed a trail down my arms, ending in our hands joined together.

"One day you'll have to show me. Just know that we all have scars. Mine are in here."

He took my right hand and placed it over his heart. I trembled under the force of his words and his unfailing stare.

"Maybe one day I will see yours and perhaps you can learn not to see mine."

"Perhaps," he answered as the clang of dishes interrupted our conversation.

"Everything okay in here?" Eliza asked.

"Yes, Mother. Everything is well."

His last word gurgled within me and nearly diminished my appetite. He'd said perhaps, which meant that for now, all he could see was my scar, regardless of his precious claim to my beauty.

It could be worse, I assured myself.

As we all took our seats around the table, Porter and his mother made easy conversation about events around the property. More food than I'd seen in a week was heaped onto my plate and after only a few bites, I was stuffed.

"Mother, I will be going away tomorrow on business. Would you mind staying here for a while longer until I get back?"

An unfounded feeling of abandonment took over, shaking me to the core. He was leaving already. He did only see my scar and was repulsed by it and by me. Unshed tears cued in the corners of my eyes and awaited their part in this tragedy of a play.

"Excuse me." I plopped my napkin down on the table and went out of the first door in sight, taking me to the living room where I spotted double doors that led outside. I opened one and slipped out, freeing myself from any further humiliation I'd caused myself. I was a fool. This wasn't a real marriage or even a fantasy of one.

His mother probably goaded him into finding a wife so that she could have grandchildren and I was just the hip-heavy sow chosen to give them to her—as soon as they fattened me up properly.

Steel yourself, Delilah.

My attention was caught by a cloud of lights in the night air—lightning bugs. They were everywhere. I took in what I could of my new home from this fresh perspective, letting it calm me. A large pond twice the size of Sable's, was at the back, complete with an island in the middle and several boats awaiting a captain. The neighs of horses could be heard in the distance. Katydids and swamp frogs made a harmonious orchestra.

I tried to take deep breaths, but the cold, humid air did nothing for my restless emotions. I had no reason to be upset.

There were worse things than living in a grand mansion with every luxury at your fingertips.

"You're upset." His voice seemed to flow in tune with the other sounds of the house as though it was also a product of this environment, made to fall into balance with the rest. I didn't expect anyone to come looking for me. Usually, when I got upset, everyone was content to leave me be. After all, they didn't want my presence in the first place.

Though a thousand responses came to mind, none exited my mouth.

"I didn't realize that I would be married today, Delilah. Please, understand. There are people that will be expecting me."

I wished that tears could be sucked back in as easily as they fell.

"It's fine," I said, straightening my posture, hoping to show him that I was unfazed by his icy repertoire. "I'm just a little overwhelmed. Of course you have better things to tend to."

If ever there was a ploy for attention that was it.

Just when I thought he'd taken his leave, I felt two warm hands on my shoulders. A shiver journeyed down my spine, alerting me to his proximity. "Not better, just business. I will be back tomorrow afternoon...unless you'd like more time to yourself."

I smiled, but tamped it down in a hurry. "We should probably get to know each other better. We are married. Anyway, I've had plenty of time to myself. I'm really not all that entertaining."

He chuckled. I felt the bass of it in the air. The weight of his body slumped against my back while his forehead leaned on the frail hairs that grew at the base of my scalp. "You're a funny one. Yes, we are married. I promise to be back as soon as I can so that we can learn more about each other."

I nodded. I was acting like a child. What did I really expect, love at first sight? Only if he was blind would that notion be so simple to wallow in.

I needed a subject change and fast.

"What should I do while you are gone? I don't really know my place here."

He began to speak. As he did, the heat of his words weaved into the back of my hair and caused every inch of me to stand at attention. "You are free here, Delilah. There may come a time when you will be able to help me with my business or find an interest of your own. We have plenty of land here and things to keep you occupied. I'm sure Mother would fill your time with her stories alone."

"I'm not one to sit around, Porter. I will find something worthy to keep me busy."

He backed away and took a few steps so that the toes of his boots hung over the edge of the porch. Crooking his neck back and forth, he grew agitated with something just out of his sight. His brown bunched right above his nose and a vein made its presence known below his ear. His jaw, structured like a statue, ground back and forth.

"Let's go inside. Please be careful out here at night. The swamp hides its secrets until we are alone."

Chapter Four

The bastard was in the trees, creeping, constantly creeping, like he always did. The fog, keeping the water company, did nothing to disguise him. If he tried any harder, squirming around, he would transform into the worm he was on the inside. All it took was the break of a twig and a whiff of his forever overpowering aftershave to know he was skulking around. He'd been trouble since before he was born and if it wasn't for the contract our families drew decades ago, he wouldn't be anywhere near me now.

The initial words that drove Marie into his arms was me warning her against it. I told her to stay away from him. I knew there was a rebellious nature about her that was constantly submerged and wanted out. I'd been warned about it by her father, her mother, and anyone else who had caught my ear.

Even his name was trouble. His mother cursed him the day she named him Rebel.

Wanting to get Delilah away from him, I took hold of her hand and went back into the house. The motion took her by surprise and she tripped over the threshold. I caught her in an awkward sideways hold. She weighed nothing and my thoughts were taken back to the measly helping she was given in her parents' home. Her skin felt boreal and again, my need to take that from her overtook any other instinct.

"Let's get you by the fire, you're cold again." Distracting her with her own discomfort was desperate, but making her aware of her new admirer would probably only fuel her curiosity.

Though Delilah didn't strike me as disloyal as Marie had been.

I was betting everything on that hunch.

I hoped against hope it was the case.

As she stepped in front of the fire, the light from the flames cast a glow on her scar and I turned out of fear that I would gasp, showing my still present shock. I'd tried. The entire day, I'd tried my best not to look at it. She was beautiful, it was true, but that scar told me so many things about her. I would've preferred to hear them from her mouth instead. The laceration screamed at me, so callous on this otherwise gentle creature. It seemed shallow to ask her to discuss trivial things when already my bond with her was tethered in something deeper than favorite colors and how early she rose in the mornings — whether I willed it or not.

There was a deep desire to protect her — a longing for her to seek her comfort from me and me alone.

"What do you do for work?" she asked. I'd thought it was common knowledge what I did. It was the reason I didn't go into the town much. Either I was asked for money or a loan. The begging was incessant.

I smothered my relief at her beginning the conversation. "My father owned several banks. I also do some investing."

She sat in the chair that she'd occupied earlier, mulling over my words. "I've tried all day to remember if we went to school together, but I couldn't remember you."

In The Rogue, all children were educated together in one classroom. After the eighth grade, it was the parents' discretion as to whether or not the child continued on. If they did, they were taught by the Constable, one of the few in the town who'd completed college on the outside.

"I was taught at home. Then I went to college on the outside."

Marie used to beg me to take her to the outside world constantly. She loved the glamour and the unabashed recklessness of the city. The more I indulged her, the more she craved it. It was like feeding an insatiable monster.

She looked at the fire, rubbing her hands together and taking in my response. "I've never been to the outside. It sounds like a horrible place. Well, they say it is anyway."

That was the typical opinion, ingrained into us from birth, of The Rogue. We were taught to fear the outside, in a strenuous effort to keep us on the inside.

"It can be. Just as The Rogue can be an awful place. Evil permeates people, no matter how well they hide."

My comment seemed to sober her. Sitting in front of a fire on a hallowed night was probably not the way she'd envisioned her honeymoon. Then again, I was probably a far cry from the quintessential husband. That was the fault in my planning. Even the money I'd paid for her hand couldn't buy her affection.

"You look worried," Delilah said, shifting her body to face me.

I didn't know how to answer her without cracking my chest open and revealing the spark of care I'd already grown for the stranger I'd been married to for less than a day.

"I tend to be a bit of a worrywart. I suppose you will have to get used to it. Like right now, for instance, I'm worried that this is all one big disappointment for you."

A flash of emotion passed over her face, causing a hue to take over her cheeks and her eyes to squint, before she corrected it. Here was my new wife and I had no idea what that face detailed or what the meaning was behind it. Those were things, I supposed, that a normal courting male would already know about his beloved.

Yet, there I sat, clueless as the day I was born.

She looked around our sitting room, taking her time to inspect each element. She must've thought us haughty and spoiled coming from where she had.

"Do you play?" Her thin finger gestured toward the plethora of instruments in the furthest corner of the room. It had been ages since I'd played for anyone. Marie had begged me to, I suspected, out of pure boredom. But by the time she did, my feelings for her had shifted from intrigue to downright hatred — yet I couldn't bring myself to end the engagement. She'd be ruined and so would her reputation.

"I do. Maybe I could play for you tomorrow." The abruptness of my offer astonished me as much as it did her, for she shifted in her chair with a jerk.

"It's been so long since I heard music — except for church service. Which one do you play?"

I turned around to assess the inventory of instruments. A violin, a viola, and the cello stood docile on their stands. "All of them—there's a record player in the library near the office as well."

"A Victrola?"

"Similar. I'll show you one day."

Her face returned to a calm stare before she turned to warm her feet. The fire's warmth easily penetrated the thin sheaths she called boots. She said nothing in response and I'd lost count of how many times I'd made a complete ass of myself.

"I have to admit, Porter, I feel a little ill-matched here. Out of place.

No answer I could give her would take away the hurt now filling her eyes. One night couldn't erase the years of degradation I'd assumed she had to put up with. She had no idea that if there was anyone not up to task in this duo, it was me. I had to try to convince her to stay. Before her, my life had become a mundane existence.

"You—you were what I needed."

The winds outside kicked up and rustled the shutters barely hanging onto the house. The flames in the fireplace danced at its bidding.

They knew a half-truth when they heard one.

Her lack of reaction to my raw confession left me wanting—yearning for her approval or at least, her understanding. Anything to make me feel like less of a good businessman and more of a husband.

One hefty exhale and she presented the gift I craved. "Sounds like fate. You needed someone and I needed a savior."

I hadn't ever really believed in fate or any other all-powerful outside force before Marie. I believed in it afterwards. I began to think that whoever it was despised me.

We both sat, not speaking.

"I've made tea, if anyone would like some."

Leave it to my mother to interrupt with more talk of food. Delilah placed her flattened hand against her belly and groaned. "I'm so grateful, but honestly, I don't think I could take a drop without bursting."

My mother and I both chuckled at her outburst. Relative to a normal person, she'd eaten a small amount, yet she was stuffed. The words she spoke were always clearly earnest. She made our home lighter. It was as though the fog that usually clung to my eyelids was blown away by her candor.

Discounting Delilah's protest, my mother placed the tray on our coffee table and began to mentally divide the servings with a pointed finger.

"This is lavender tea. It will calm your nerves and allow you a good night's sleep. Humor an old woman."

Guilt was my mother's specialty. Delilah shot me a look that begged me to intervene or to at least sympathize, but on that particular point, I had to agree. My wife was skin and bones and if anyone saw her, they'd think I was abusive or neglectful. Though the depth of The Rogue's sins reached hell itself, the blatant abuse of a woman was frowned upon—though no one, it seemed, had intervened in Delilah's parents' neglect.

The hypocrisy of a society birthed upon a high moral compass was infuriating.

The only sympathy Delilah got from me was a shrug.

"Just a tiny bit, please."

My mother filled her cup to the edge, almost overflowing.

We sipped our tea in quiet, allowing the outside sounds to fill the air. Mother's eyes roamed from me to Delilah more than once, prompting me to say something—but nothing came. I had plenty of questions, but the silence seemed to have a calming effect that surpassed the tea. Her tea cup resting in her lap, only minutes later, Delilah's eyes drooped. Minute by minute, her awareness faded. The fire in the hearth mirrored her, dying down a little with each fall of her eyelids. The teacup tipped and threatened to fall. I reached for her cup and took it without a flinch from her direction.

"You've stuffed her into exhaustion."

A giggle from my mother waived off my accusation.

"Take her to bed, poor stick of a girl. Give me two weeks tops and those frilly dresses you've purchased will have to be let out for sure."

With one arm under her knees and one behind her back, I gathered Delilah against my chest and began to carry her to her bedroom — our bedroom. As we ascended the stairs, her right hand fisted the front of my shirt and the faint movement melted me. Peace brandished her sleep in the depth of her breaths.

Like this, with the left side of her face against me, I couldn't see the roughness of her life played out along her jaw.

She was beautiful, it was true, but that line just took center stage.

"Maybe," she whispered in a voice that could easily be the mouthpiece of heaven. Her raven lashes fluttered and her eyes moved as if the person she was dreaming of was approaching her.

"Maybe what?" I whispered back, my mind shackled with a tormenting need to know what she was dreaming of, or who.

"Don't hope," she breathed and her voice carried a tone of exasperation. My steps faltered with her words. If she was telling herself or someone else not to hope, it meant that hope was present. Hope was a privilege I'd given up on a long time ago.

I laid her down in the bed a few seconds later, making sure to remove the pathetic excuses for shoes from her feet and stoking the fire in her room. The comforter was tucked around her and she turned and embraced the damned thing. One day, she would reach for me in her sleep.

Before leaving, I drew the curtains closed. It was in tugging on the last curtain that my nightmare came to full fruition outside, startling me. I didn't know if I'd actually called out in fear or whether it was just in my head, but turning around and seeing no movement from Delilah; I knew it was silent.

My once dear Marie stood outside in her juvenile form, floating in the distance.

She seemed to make herself known more and more. I supposed it didn't bother me much. If I wasn't careful, her image would scare me a little from time to time.

But other than her nagging and whining, Marie had never hurt a fly.

Chapter Five

I woke to an empty bed, but I didn't know why it surprised me. Sleeping by myself was as normal as the sunrise itself. I knew Porter would be gone and even if he was still here, he wouldn't be here with me. What surprised me was that I lamented the loss.

The sun was still conversing with the branches of the Cypress trees outside when I looked through the window. A singing rooster welcomed the morning somewhere far away.

I almost expected to see my little phantom friend outside, waiting to haunt me again, but I saw nothing short of a normal breathtaking morning.

Then again, anything was breathtaking in comparison to where I'd woken up the day before.

I washed up in the sink after only three attempts at getting the water to turn on. Calendula soap tickled my nose and made me sneeze. My poor nose was used to filth and ashes—none of the flower smelling stuff.

I sighed looking at my choices for dress. As if I didn't stand apart among the rich furnishings of the home already, my clothes were even more worn looking than the cook. I was like a rotting rose in a bouquet of fresh cut daisies. Then again, I was downright afraid of what Porter had chosen.

"Did you look at the things Porter bought for you? I'm not sure if they will fit, but we tried."

My mother-in-law was a mind reader.

Her hand was laid on my shoulder. Still not accustomed to the touch of others so often, I twitched and then relaxed.

"I looked a bit yesterday, but was overwhelmed. He really shouldn't have."

"Come, it's all in the wardrobe. We can fill up the closet later."

Eliza threw open both doors of the tall mahogany wardrobe and revealed more dresses and clothing than I'd ever owned in my life—maybe in mine and my sisters' lives combined. A tear flickered in my eye at the sight. I knew that I was pawned off to the first person who had shown interest, but Porter was showing me kindness beyond my station—beyond what I deserved.

"Oh, don't you cry. You'll make me cry. Look at these. Maybe if I didn't stuff my gullet with breads, I could fit in tiny clothes like this too." She saw my hesitation in touching the garments. It was like my hands weren't fit to hold them. "Pick the first outfit that you see, the first thing that catches your eye."

A skirt the color of a dehydrated oak leaf hung the lowest and I fingered the edges, thinking that I'd never seen material that looked so soft, it must've been illusion.

"There is a matching corset as well." Eliza noticed my attraction to the skirt and began flitting through the hangers, looking for its lover. "Here, it matches the black shirt and the cream-colored one. Which one would you like?"

I was tired of wearing black and gray as if in perpetual funeral garb.

"The cream, please."

"I…" Eliza stuttered, handing over my new clothes and now pulling my hair at the ends. "I could fix your hair. I've never had a daughter. It would give me such joy."

"I've never had someone who wanted to fix my hair, so we are even. Give me a moment to dress and then my hair is yours."

With a clap and a giggle, she exited the room. If Porter was to be gone often, I would need to make friends with the woman who shared a connection to him. It was imperative.

Avoiding the mirror, I stepped back into the bathroom and put on the clothes. It didn't skip my notice that I'd slept in the same clothes I'd arrived in which meant that I didn't even remember putting myself to bed. I must've been exceptionally tired.

My clothes were a little large, even after the tightening of the corset. I felt exposed without my threadbare shawl.

"Is there a shawl or something to cover my shoulders?" The question was posed as I opened the door to my mother-in-law, now pacing in front of the doors.

"Of course. There's also a cloak. I thought maybe you'd like to take a walk around the property before breakfast. Be alone with your thoughts a bit. You seem like the kind of girl who appreciates a few breaths alone."

"I would appreciate that very much. Thank you."

"Now, sit at your vanity. Let me see what I've been missing with only a son."

I sat down on the pillow-seated chair but chose to look down at the trinkets that decorated the surface instead of the mirror. Eliza chose the brush with delicate ornamental paintings of ladies getting ready for the day brushed onto the head. Her strokes were kind and gentle, and I actually found it pleasant. The task of fixing my hair had always been in my own hands and it wasn't until I was older that I procured a method to the madness, saving both my sanity and my scalp.

"You've got some dry spots at the ends. Would you mind if I cut a few inches?"

It wasn't as if a few inches was the river between me and beautiful.

"Of course. Do what you wish."

Minutes later, Eliza beckoned me to look. She'd rolled and braided my dense black curls into a work of art that almost took away from the ridged mark on my face.

"Thank you." I attempted to show her a decent amount of enthusiasm for her effort, but my tone fell flat in delivering.

"Here." She passed a burgundy cloak to me from the wardrobe. I took it, letting the fabric caress my shoulders and give me the protection I desired. It was more a matter of modesty than warmth. It offered me a sense of protection. Just for added warmth, I put on a black open cardigan underneath.

"I won't be long. I will be afraid of getting lost."

"Take your time. We will keep breakfast ready."

Words I'd never heard before.

After a quick hello to the staff who were diligent for such an early hour, I snuck out the back door. For a moment, I was content with the scene before me. Long gone was the spooky pond that seemed to hold secrets of its own. In its place was a scene straight out of a Jane Austen novel. The still water now beckoned. The boats didn't seem ghost-infested — simply lonely. Another look across the property revealed an expanse I wouldn't have ever seen in the pitch black of night. Though the gardens were now bare, in my mind's eye, I could imagine what they'd once looked like, fresh and alive with promise. Now they matched the rest of the estate, a self-telling tale of splendor that once was.

No matter how dreary the place seemed, the birds didn't care. The swamp sparrows could be heard singing their good mornings and an egret's wings flapped in the distance.

Just as I'd resigned myself to waiting for a tour from Porter, a horse's neigh drew my attention. I walked off of the back porch and down the steps, headed in the direction of the sound. A song rose from the worn down barn, its baritone comfort caused shivers down my spine as I approached.

"Who is there?" I called out, wanting to meet the owner of such a voice.

I got closer and closer. As I did the song seemed to digress into a solemn cry for pity. It beckoned me like a siren.

"Hello?" I repeated my inquiry, hoping not to have to go into the horse stables with my new clothing and boots on. Porter had gone to a lot of trouble to get me those clothes and I intended on cherishing them.

"Who is it?" The once soulful bellowing now barked at me.

"I am Delilah, Porter's wife." I tested my tongue with my teeth after saying such a thing aloud.

"Hold on." More barking.

I pulled the cloak tighter around myself, the humidity now turning the air colder even with the morning sun coming into her own.

Porter had spoken of a stable boy, but the bass that boasted from the inside of the decrepit barn sounded like no boy I'd ever know. It was more like caramel wrapped in warm honey that reverberated through my chest.

While I waited for the stranger to make his appearance, the wind echoed through the trees. If I didn't know better, I would think they were whispering secrets to one another in haste.

"I didn't know I was singing for an audience. I would've practiced harder."

I gasped at the nearness of the voice and to whom it was attached. His breath could be felt on my neck and the warmth caused a shiver to ripple down my back and come to a dead end in my toes. I tucked the shawl around my knuckles and gripped it tight, hoping it would magically turn to steel and form a solid barrier between me and this thief of breath. A necklace hung around his neck and the locket at the bottom of it hung out of his shirt where he'd neglected to button it. As soon as he caught me looking at it, he stuffed it back into his shirt with haste and tended to the forgotten buttons.

In his hands, he dangled a handwritten list of things to get done, one that had nothing crossed off.

"Who—who are you?" I stammered out. The cold of the morning turned my words to tiny clouds that puffed out before me.

"Forgive my manners," the boy, clad in brown pants and a khaki shirt only halfway tucked beneath worn suspenders said. "I'm Rebel. You must be Porter's new wife." I didn't answer quick enough for him and so he continued. "No? Another servant like me? It is certainly my lucky day." With the word lucky, he took the opportunity to close in one more step toward me, but I took the same opportunity to recover the space between us with my own step back.

"I am Porter's wife."

He smiled. The corners of his mouth spread so wide that I thought maybe they'd touch his earlobes with little help. "Is that your name then? Porter's wife." What was once a polite tone, turned snide and irritated. A fish bubbled the surface of the pond in the distance, but with my senses on high alert, I heard it loud and clear.

"My name is Delilah."

There was no reply to my sudden firm stance. His left eyebrow pulsed a little at my name but that was the only indication that he'd heard me at all.

"Delilah, huh?" His hazel eyes sparkled with mischief and it made the hairs on the back of my neck stand at attention. "Well, just so you know, no matter how…" his eyes roamed my form, never halting until they were once again on my face. "…lovely you are or how much you charm me — I'll never tell you the source of my power. Not even for a touch of those luscious lips."

My legs threatened to topple. Rebel's words wove around my core. Curiosity flourished in my veins and though my conscience pulled me away, I stayed, my eyes fixed on his. By mistake, I looked down at his lips, rounded and perfect, and saw the sheen of sweat marked the top.

"What's a flit like you wandering around for? Has Porter decided to loosen the leash already?"

Through the experiences of my life, I'd learned to be slow to offense. I was the last one to be stricken by insult — until now. I'd been called a myriad of hellacious names in my short life, but a leashed beast was not one I'd ever been called by my worst enemy.

Without another word to the horrid male, I turned around and set off on a path toward the house. I chastised myself the entire way back for not waiting for Porter to accompany me. Only seconds in the presence of that man and a thousand worms crawled across my skin; at the same time I felt like a harlot. Though I didn't care for his directness, there was something so forward about the way he stated his intentions. There were no secrets or masks of gentlemanly virtue.

The plain intrigue he'd stirred made me look back to the barn more than once only to find Rebel, hands on hips, staring after me.

The knowledge that he was looking at me with such ardent fervor made me quicken my steps. Before I knew it, I was back inside the safety of my new home with furniture and food beyond my means. Even the cypress flooring I stood upon was better than my station.

"Delilah, that wasn't much of a walk. Oh, dear, you look flushed. Is everything okay?"

I took a breath, purposefully removing my shawl at a snail's pace to collect myself. My mind told me I'd overreacted to Rebel's presence. It couldn't be helped. There was an air of knowing about him that slithered over my skin—and intrigued me more than I was willing to admit.

"Yes. I took a turn that led me around by the barn. Then, I was lost for a moment. The stable boy pointed me back home."

What a fragile lie. Not only was the lie a complete shamble, but it made me sound like a pathetic twit — getting lost when this house was big enough to be seen for at least a half a mile.

"Hmmmm, next time, Porter will be around. Maybe it's best if he accompanies you from now on."

While she spoke, she seemed to be scanning my face and neck for evidence of something. With that boy's voice, the one that crawled along my skin like molasses, she was probably checking for hickeys.

My sister had returned home one night with hickeys when she was supposed to have been going to tutoring.

My mother had congratulated her.

"Yes, I suppose so."

"But," she threaded her arm through my elbow and pulled me along, "I bet it was enough to rustle up your hunger." There was no real question, but I nodded in response, anyway. This woman's insatiable appetite seemed to be the revolving theme of the day — everyday. "We usually have breakfast in the kitchen. It's easier for clean-up and Porter only ever has coffee. Anyway, June likes the way the sunlight comes in through the bay window. If we keep the help happy, we don't have to worry about spittle in our soup."

She laughed as I suppressed a gag. I made a mental note not to ever eat soup again unless I'd watched it be prepared.

"June, look who I found!" Eliza may as well have danced through the kitchen as though finding me was a prize. She talked to June as an old friend.

If my mother had talked to me with half the heart that Eliza spoke to June, my heart would've never longed for anything more.

"I'm so glad you could join us. We need fresh gossip at this table," June said. Her words rose and fell like humming. June was a plump woman, but not like Eliza. She was solid and thick — there were muscles in her arms that would rival any mans. She must've worked very hard for the family.

I took her passive suggestion into account.

I felt like this was a test. If I participated in the gossip, I would look like a sinner — gossip was always admonished from the pulpit. But if I didn't participate, I'd never fit in with these two women who were tethered to my new life's happiness.

I sat down and smiled, choosing the path more traveled.

"It's amazing what you hear while washing others' clothes."

Eliza looked shocked, grabbing her ample bosom and gasping. "You worked? What kind of father makes his daughter work at such laborious endeavors?"

"Mine. And yes, I washed clothes for three households."

June sighed as she placed the last platter of shrimp and grits out on the table. "The only gossip we get around here is secondhand from Porter. And it's from the outside, so we don't understand half of the things he speaks of. He always returns with a smile on his face though, and that's worth the time away."

If the outside was such a dastardly place, then what about it made Porter happy?

"I would love to hear some stories," I spoke up. "They're all new to me. I know nothing about the outside."

Before I could serve myself, a massive dollop of the savory shrimp was piled on my plate along with grits, eggs, and a stone of a biscuit. This was the first of many choices that were taken from me that morning. Eventually, I simply sat back and allowed Eliza to dress up the already elaborate choices on my plate with butter, jellies, and salt.

I had more condiments on my plate than I usually had actual food.

For the rest of the meal, I listened to the now third-hand stories of Porter and the world that I'd never known. June and Eliza told them with such gusto that a stranger would've thought they were speaking of a conquistador and his conquests.

I skirted my food around the plate for the most part, using the empty spaces as proof that I'd at least attempted to eat my fill. My stomach became jittery at my second cup of coffee and added to my nervousness which never seemed to vanish.

This morning I was allowed to help with the dishes and the cleaning. Without Porter around, the chores seemed more communal and less like the owner and the help. Everyone was freer in spirit in his absence.

Except me—there was no denying my longing for his presence.

I felt exposed without Porter's shadow.

"What do we do the rest of the day?" I posed the question to both of the women in the kitchen who, to me, were on equal footing.

"Well, I need to go to town to visit the butcher. We need more ham and then something for supper." June's answer was swift.

"And I—what do I do, June?" Eliza turned to June who was already set on completing her task, grabbing a coat and tying a well-made bonnet on her head.

"Today, you're embroidering my new handkerchiefs and you eat a lot."

My eyes bugged out while both of the women chuckled at the dig—an open joke to them.

"Oh, Delilah, I'm not offended. I'm quite proud of my robust appetite."

"Robust — there's a fitting word."

This time, I joined in the fun. Until a low-drummed clearing of the throat interrupted our fun. Everything in my from the heat in my belly to the tingling in my chest knew it was him. The atmosphere in the room hummed with a looming seriousness — even the ceiling moaned at the swift metamorphosis.

I turned around to face my new husband and expected the happiness that visiting the outside was told to have brought him. He was breathtaking. He wore a suit, but the fashion was nothing that I'd ever seen in The Rogue. The seams were crisp, the lines were precise and well-tailored — nothing compared to his rattily stitched pants of the day before.

Everything about him was so exact, it was as though he was crafted by a machine.

But there was no smile or even a sliver of happiness to go with all of the well put together man in front of me. My heart shriveled at the knowing. Of course he wasn't happy anymore — I was what he had to come home to now.

He would probably never return home happy ever again.

Those women—the women who relied on that happiness should've been warned. Beware ladies, this is the last time I will be happy—enjoy it.

"Not a good trip?" Eliza brought forth the obvious.

"It was a good trip. Everything was handled pretty fast. That's why I was able to come home early."

He spoke to his mother—I'd realized that he reserved a special tone just for her and while he used that tone, his eyes never left mine.

Breakfast curdled and coiled in my stomach, revolting against the death of my surety that this marriage would be okay—maybe even good.

"That's excellent. Can we get you anything? Coffee?"

"Coffee would be great. Thank you."

My eyes left his stare and darted around the room in desperate search of somewhere to hide. He made me feel translucent.

I shivered as I found no prospects and against my better judgment looked at him again. Something stewed within him.

"Are you well today, wife?"

How was it that one word could hold two very different connotations? When he called me wife in the shadows of this overwhelming home, it felt like a promise. But when he called me wife just a second before, it felt impersonal—out of touch.

"I am well, and you?"

I knew how he was. He didn't have to tell me.

"I'm cold. The wind has picked up. It's a shame. I thought we'd take a tour of the property today, but I wouldn't want you to get sick."

His words aggravated me.

"Let's go into the sitting room. There's a good fire in there."

I was going through the motions, returning the kindness from the night before. I didn't know how to be a decent wife any more than he knew how to be a husband. I hadn't had a good example, so winging it was the best I had.

He walked in a taxed manner, his steps half the gait of what I'd remembered.

"Would you like to lie down? Or I could get you something to eat."

He sat at the chair that was much bigger than the other and scooted the smaller chair closer to the fire. At first, I thought it was for me, but then he shucked his shoes and one by one perched his feet up, wiggling his toes.

I wrung my hands, waiting for his answer.

"Have you eaten?"

"I have."

"I don't like to eat alone. I'm fine here. Thank you."

I found a stool with a pincushion top and dragged it closer. June brought in a tray with coffee and despite his denial, he ate the biscuits that she brought as well.

"You ate." I praised the effort.

"I wasn't alone."

I waited a few more moments before broaching the subject I was most interested in at that moment. "What is this fashion?"

I waved an arm, gesturing toward his suit, so strange to me, yet completely attractive on my husband.

"This is what businessmen wear on the outside. I didn't have a chance to change. I wanted to get home as soon as possible."

I didn't ask why and I didn't have to. At my next breath, his rough hand was on my cheek. His knuckles skimmed along my face before tucking a stray hair behind my ear. I was breathless against the motion. It warmed me from face to feet, never faltering.

"Why?" The word tumbled from my mouth without permission. Inherently knowing his meaning wasn't good enough for me. I wouldn't insinuate anything in this case. I needed to hear the words—even if they weren't what I'd assumed.

"Because I have a new wife that I hardly know."

"What would you want to know of your new wife?"

He looked at the fire and pulled off the jacket, then loosening the long tie around his neck.

"Anything — everything."

"It will be a short conversation."

He ignored my quip. "How many siblings do you have?"

"I have two, Adele and Elaine. They are both married."

"I had one brother, a baby who died at six months old." A clap of thunder rumbled outside, as if the clouds were angry with him for bringing it up.

"He was in a high chair and he kicked against the table and hit the back his head on the buffet. His grave is in the back. I'll show you one day."

I stretched my back, relieving it of the curved posture that came with sitting on the tiny stool. "Come sit up here. I think this chair is yours now, anyway. It never fit anyone here." He took his feet down. The seat was overwarm from being next to the fire.

"And your father?"

He fisted the thigh of his pants. "He died of a heart attack. His appetite put mother's to shame. We are supposed to be talking about you."

I pouted my lip and his eyes targeted the motion with great interest. "I have to learn about you too."

He smiled. "Yes, that's true. What did you do this morning?"

"I took a walk around the grounds, but not far—just to the barn."

Porter stiffened with my words. "Was anyone out there?"

"Yes. Rebel? He must be the stable boy."

"He's supposed to be the stable boy. He's very good at avoiding his job. Did he say anything to you?"

"Not much."

Rebel had said plenty to me, both in speech and movement, but I didn't want to alarm Porter. Our conversation flattened after the mention of Rebel. The only noises in the house were his breathing and the crackle of the fire. I wanted to find out more about him, but there had to be a better way than this ridiculous back and forth.

I reverted back to the only thing I knew well. There was a lot a person could infer about another person's choice of books—if there were any here.

"Do you have any books?"

"Yes. In the library that connects with my office. You're welcome to read anything from there. Consider them yours."

I stood and started in the direction of the office before I hesitated. Enclosing myself in a library wouldn't do anything to further what he'd returned home for in such haste. I had to make an effort even if it meant gathering every speck of bravery I owned.

I held out a shaking hand toward him. "Aren't you coming with me?"

Porter looked taken aback and though he'd nodded, he didn't move to follow through with the agreement.

Come on girl, you can do this.

I reached out both of my hands and grabbed his. He still looked stupefied but got my drift, rising to stand in front of me.

"How about I go change out of this suit and I'll meet you in the library shortly?"

"Sure." With all my effort to be forward, I'd failed. It was this damned scar. All he saw was the scar. All he would ever see was the scar.

I looked down at myself and snickered. No amount of new clothing could change a face.

With a sigh, I made my way upstairs, grabbing a blanket from the end of my bed and dragging it with me to his office. True to his word, through a side door, was a pristine library, filled to the brim with hard-covered beauties just waiting to be discovered. My excitement was soon squashed as I began to read the titles on the first shelf. Accounting, business, and finance was the running theme.

Nothing to get lost in.

"Remind me to use those as firewood one day." I turned and gasped. "Believe me, the disgust for those boring encyclopedias is mutual. The good ones are over here."

This time he took my hand and pulled me to the other side of the room which, strangely, had a different smell in addition to a juxtaposed list of titles. It was like we'd stumbled into a parallel universe.

"These are my mother's books. Don't read the back matter unless you're ready for a shock. I learned most of what I know about women from sneaking in here to read those books when I was a teenager. I used to hide one of her books inside an open copy of one of those books." He pointed to the books of disdain.

"You were a mischievous one," I remarked, thumbing through the titles not on the brazen bookshelf.

"I did my fair share. What about you? Any misbehavior I should be aware of?"

I laughed, but there was no comedy in it. "This is what I got for just being obedient; imagine my fate if I'd been defiant. I may not have limbs." Porter cringed. Sometimes I forgot how my scar affected others, other than the obvious pity. "I'm sorry."

"You're apologizing for someone marring this beautiful face?""

His Haunted Heart

My heart thrummed in my head, blocking out everything else but its rhythm. My defenses came and went as fast as two beats while the flood of a blush washed over my face.

"I apologize for everything. It seems to keep me out of trouble."

"Well, now you can practice *not* apologizing. I doubt you'll ever do anything that warrants one, anyway."

He squatted down and searched in earnest for a specific title, growing more and more tenacious when he didn't find it. I brushed past him, forgoing the elicit titles for the more tame classics and stumbled upon Jane Eyre. It was one of my favorites. The teacher had snuck it into my bag one day at school. Though I was exhausted at night, I managed to sneak in a few pages every time I could. It took me nearly a year to read through the entire volume.

I cried over the death of Helen like it was my own friend.

"Rochester is an ass," Porter called, still in his place, but peeking over his shoulder at my choice.

"He's tormented. There's a difference."

"So he's excused?"

"He's not excused, just misunderstood. Broody is becoming on some people."

He chuckled. The sound rumbled through the space, bouncing off the walls. The whole place filled with the boom.

"Maybe I should try to be broody."

I snapped the book shut and spun on my heels. "Too late."

This time we laughed together.

Chapter Six

Porter

We'd spent the whole day together. It hadn't been my intention, but the surprise was pleasant. By the time dinner time came around, as we sat across from each other at the table, she'd blossomed like a flower, no longer holding her petals tight.

Though every time she smiled, her eyes looked downward.

And a funny-shaped dimple concaved on the left side of her mouth.

I tried, in vain, to ignore my mother looking back and forth between us.

"Delilah, dear," she interrupted my unabashed stare. "Did you tell Porter about your little ghostly sighting?"

I dropped my fork and then tried to recover my folly by coughing. It was futile.

"I did not."

"Well, maybe it's something you can tell him about later on."

"Sure." Delilah answered. The petals fell back into place around her.

The rest of the meal was taken in silence.

"Do you want to go for a walk with me tonight?" I offered, with a hidden agenda.

"Yes. Let me get my cloak."

After she was up the stairs and out of sight, I retrieved my bags from the porch where I'd left them. While she'd slept the night before, I searched her boots and found the number eight worn down, almost unreadable.

"I'm ready now."

"You cannot wear those boots outside. They won't protect you from anything." It was a chore to force my face to remain stern.

"I'm sorry," she whispered, knocking the toes of the boots together. "These are all I have."

"Then it's a good thing I bought these." From behind my back, I pulled a brand new pair of boots. I'd bought four different pair in varying shades and skins. She would find that out later, tonight this pair would do.

"Porter, you didn't. You've given me too much already."

Her eyes betrayed her words, gazing at the boots.

"I have done no such thing. You're offending me. Come, put them on."

With a great deal of slowness, she reached me. As her lithe hands grabbed the boots, I held on, teasing her a bit for her protest. "Porter..." she said with a bit of groan.

"Hurry, I know a place where the lightning bugs roam."

"I'm hurrying."

One by one she clunked the decrepit boots to the side. "Let's throw those to the trash."

She smiled and for the second time that day, I saw her run her pointer finger down the length of her nose. I would have to pay more attention, but I already assumed it was an endearing quirk.

"That's where I found them in the first place. It would be like returning them home."

"You found them in the trash?"

She picked them up lovingly. "I did. They served me well. Some of the best things are those that others feel need to be discarded."

Another run of her finger down her nose. The quick move was now so obviously her outward sign of embarrassment.

After setting the boots outside the front door, she laced her arm through mine after some coercion. We walked for hours, unfazed by the lack of light or the looming darkness. She didn't seem to scare easily at the things most women, and namely Marie, used to shy away from.

"Where are you taking me?"

The moon threw streams of light down on her hair, making the blackness turn to blue. Her pale skin was luminescent and it took everything in me not to reach out and touch her face again. Throughout the day I'd felt that if I didn't steal even the smallest touch, that I might crumble.

"It's right up here."

Within minutes we came upon the biggest cypress tree on the lands. I'd been drawn to it since I was a child and demanded that a platform be built upon it. Many hours I had spent on that throne of my own, away from the world below, with my dreams in the clouds above me, playing out fantasies of lore and books unwritten.

"Climb up," I offered, remembering my manners.

"I'm in a skirt, Porter."

"I won't look, I swear."

She looked up the length of the ladder and then back to me, quelling a smile. "Put your face on the trunk of this tree and don't look until I tell you, okay?"

"Sounds like a game of hide and seek."

Raising her nose to snub me, she replied, "That's my offer, take it or leave it."

A furious blush marked her cheeks when she got a little cheeky — probably the first time she'd been allowed to let her true colors shine.

I waited a breath to agree. Her premise was understood and it was too soon to ask for her trust.

"I'll accept your terms. But you owe me. You do know the rules about owing me, don't you?"

A hand on her hip and a cut of her eyes — she knew the rules for sure. I could call in her debt anytime I wanted.

With my forehead pressed against the rugged bark of the tree, I waited for her to ascend to the place I'd once called my second home, though it was little more than stray wood nailed into a tree.

"You can look now, Porter."

Warmth radiated in my chest when she said my name. I made my way up the board nailed to the trunk, my makeshift ladder, until I reached the top. The stars shone brighter up here and the air was filtered, only allowing the purest of breaths and the clearest of dreams. The fog could be seen below, hovering, waving its hands over the surface of the pond, casting a cotton blanket over the land.

And my wife, she was almost brand new to me here. Well, she was still new, but getting to know her was a joy — not the hassle I'd imagined. She swayed back and forth while perched on the edge of the unkempt flat, staring at the lightning bugs in the distance. A finger drew lines in the air, moving from one to the other. She was either drawing an invisible picture or counting them.

By the light of the moon, she was no longer someone I tasked with saving my life or ridding me of my loneliness. She was beautiful, inside and out.

"How many?" I asked, guessing that she was, in fact, counting them.

Her shoulders sagged and a giggle escaped her mouth. "I lost count."

"My fault?"

She shook her head. "No. I got distracted by their beauty. This place seems like a dream. The fog, the lights in the sky — like I stumbled into a fairy tale."

After a length of overthinking, I put my arm around her back and barely touched her waist. Delilah stiffened beside me and I thought I'd made a dire mistake.

Until she scooted closer, resting her head on my shoulder.

"How often do you leave?" she asked in a whisper.

"Sometimes once or twice a week. Sometimes, I have to stay for longer trips."

I valued my trips away from The Rogue when I was engaged to Marie. Her constant nagging to go with me to buy her clothes, more clothes, and baubles than anyone ever needed, made it a vacation from my life and the fiancé that was more like an anchor than a sail.

"Would you want to go with me sometime?"

The proposition was out of my mouth before I could rein it in.

She backed off enough to look me in the face but still remained in the circle of my arm. "Why?"

"Why not?" I countered. "You're my wife. My mother used to travel with my father. It's a bit of a shock to the system the first few times. You don't have to—I just thought…"

She resumed her previous posture. It wasn't a yes, but it wasn't a no, either.

"Would I have to wear different clothes?"

I sighed. Most of the women of the outside weren't kept to the older standards that women of The Rogue were. If the Constable or any male saw a woman dressed inappropriately, she would be reprimanded at once. Even the women who were known to work at The Plots dressed in a pious manner in comparison to those on the outside world.

I would be the first to admit that the outside had a magnetism. The underlying slither of sinful freedom became a pull. I drank alcohol in the outside world, which was forbidden here. I smoked cigars and watched movies that made my mother's books seem like nursery rhymes.

Nausea rolled through my stomach at the thought of Delilah in that world. Her innocence and purity was something I'd expected, but over the course of the day I, had learned to cherish it. Delilah was how The Rogue began — she was this innocence that the founders had hidden away from the world to protect.

My arm tightened around her waist at the thought of someone taking that away — dimming that iridescence I saw in her that I hadn't seen in someone for a long time.

It was my charge to protect it — to protect her.

"Let's forget about it for now. I've handled everything so that I could stay here for a week or so. There's no rush for you to make a decision."

"A week is a long time."

"Is it? I bet it goes by like a flash. Today certainly did."

Movement in the distance caught my eye and I knew what it was before bringing it into focus. Just like her lover, Marie lurked in the distance, under trees, below the cover of rain. She'd always been a coward, but it had become worse in death. She had always appeared to me as a small child in her ghost form. I chalked it up to her obsession with age and beauty. If she was young in her after-life, then her shallow fears of growing old and growing ugly would never come to fruition.

"You're going to think me mad," Delilah breathed next to me.

"What?"

"Do you see her too?"

She didn't point, but her eyes told me where she looked.

"I see her every once in a while." The fact that twice in one day Delilah had seen Marie scared me more than I had been the first time I'd seen the ghost for myself. She didn't do much to me, simply floated around the grounds.

"She changes." My wife intonated the fact like she still didn't believe her eyes. And I couldn't believe my ears. I didn't understand how Marie was appearing to Delilah or why.

"How?"

A shiver caused me to quake. I didn't like that my former life and the one that I'd chosen were intersecting.

"I first saw her when you were at my door—at my parent's house. She was not more than a year old, standing in the rain. The second time was in the foyer, right inside the door. That was yesterday. She was a little older, maybe three or so. I could see right through her."

I leaned my face against her hair. She smelled like lilacs and lavender and I took the opportunity to breathe her in. "Why didn't you tell me? Weren't you frightened?"

"Eliza was there. She said it was an older property. I thought things like that may happen all the time. And it was hours after our wedding. I didn't want you to think you'd married a mental case."

"Look at me, Delilah."

Her thin body turned, but her eyes remained downcast. I placed my finger under her chin and tipped it gently, wanting to see her eyes when I told her. Finally her gaze traveled the length of my face until landing right where I wanted it to be. Her eyelashes were killer—making the brilliance of the blue come to life.

"Delilah, I want you to know that you are safe with me. If this is going to work, we can have no lies or secrets. I've seen enough around here not to be surprised by anything you have to say. I know your life has been filled with strife, but I will protect you as best I can."

My body begged me to hold on to her closer, to press her against my chest and feel her heartbeat next to mine.

"I've kept secrets all my life."

I sighed and thought of a way to get someone who barely knew me to believe what I had to say. "But we give those things up when we enter a marriage. Nothing you can say will make me forsake you—nothing."

I let the notion settle with both of us. She'd agreed with a nod of the head, but the proof would reveal itself in the coming days.

Delilah resembled a fairy, dangling her legs back and forth over the edge—the slight wind fueling the dance of several strands of hair around her face. Her tomorrow eyes never missed a thing, flitting back and forth across the sky, considering every object that I'd taken for granted.

A smile tipped at the corner of my mouth. She was exquisite beyond anything I'd ever known could be.

There was no scar in this light—only her.

"I almost forgot. I have something for you."

"You've given me so much. Please, not another thing."

"This one is more for me than you." Her face canted, her doubt evident. "I'm serious. This one proves that we are married. It will relieve me of the guilt I carry for not bringing it to the church."

I slipped two rings from my pocket. One was my father's and one was my grandmother's. The ring I intended to give my rose-faced bride was an antique. Its vintage styling was simple, yet elegant. A silver band met in a love knot underneath a sapphire. The color bowed in shame to the color of Delilah's eyes. I presented it to her on an open hand, the only packaging I had.

If I could've, I would've opened up my heart and offered it to her as well.

Her gasp told me nothing. Marie had gasped as well, but hers was a gasp of repulsion. The ring wasn't new or gold—expectations I hadn't adhered to.

"You don't like it." I came to the conclusion right away.

"I love it, Porter. It's the most beautiful ring I've ever seen." Her voice didn't falter—her words rang true.

Her fingers, cold and slim, shook when I took her hand and pushed the ring onto her finger. The fit was perfect.

"I have one too," I told her for no good reason.

I showed it to her for a brief second and then fit it over the top of my finger to show her my commitment to the deal we were silently making for the second time.

"No, let me." Her eyes widened.

"Sure."

She pushed it into my ring finger and then turned it around a few times for good measure. I thought to call in my favor—to ask her to taste the lips that I'd watched talk and laugh the whole day through.

No, I would hold onto it.

Because when and if Delilah Jeansonne ever kissed me it would be of her own free will.

Chapter Seven

The first thing I felt the next morning was not the pull of a yawn in my throat or the sting of morning's first light — it was the new weight wound around my ring finger.

I'd been afraid to breathe too heavily the night before of fear that it might just all fall apart.

I stayed under the covers with my eyes closed, allowing the fantasy to relive itself in my mind over and over until the promise of the day's events pried me from them.

Excuse after excuse popped into my head, explaining and rationalizing his behavior — his words — the glint in his eyes.

He was drunk.

He was caught in a fit of temporary insanity.

He'd been infected by the plague and the fever was frying his brain.

It went on and on until I'd convinced myself it was all a farce.

I'd mentally declared it was time to put my thoughts aside and rise from the bed, determined to make this day anew instead of merely trying to extend that night.

That's when I felt it. A touch on my hand, so light and gentle that if not for the coldness it contained, I would've blamed it on a draft. My body stilled — including my heart.

My eyes roamed the room against the will of my body, searching for the owner of a touch that could chill me to the bone. I saw nothing. Bits of dust floated in the air, the sunlight peering through the splice in the curtains making it look like tiny angels.

Yet no one was in my room and nothing could explain the touch I'd felt.

A giggle broke free of my mouth; what a silly thing to get scared over. The sheets had probably just brushed over the top of my hand.

I heard noises below, making me think the house helpers were busy with their day. It made me feel lazy and useless.

After choosing an empire-waist burgundy dress, I pulled open the wardrobe to get my new boots. Next to them were almost a half-dozen other pairs, all in different colors and skins.

This was ridiculous.

Porter was spoiling the wrong girl.

I chose the same pair of boots he'd given me the night before in order to circumvent a discussion about them. This way I could pretend that I hadn't seen the others.

I just hoped to God that he didn't ask me. I wasn't a very good liar.

After brushing out my hair and bundling it into a bun that made a few locks fall along the side of my face, I walked downstairs, bound and determined to make myself useful, setting my childish fantasies aside for the third time that morning.

Pushing open the swinging door between the entryway and the kitchen, I heard the voices of my breakfast company from the day before.

"There she is. Just in time." I denied the flop of my heart at the absence of Porter. A good night's sleep had probably woken him up and cleared his head.

Or his fever broke.

Or he took a pill for his temporary insanity.

"I'm sorry. I slept a little too well."

Though I was told that my mother in law would be leaving the day after we were married, I was glad she'd never left.

Eliza patted my shoulder and handed me a platter of breakfast, gesturing with her finger for me to bring it to the dining room. I ate in silence, sipping the lemony tea made entirely too sweet for my taste and listening to the chatter of the older women of the house.

"He doesn't eat breakfast. It's just his way."

I looked up to find June had predicted the reason for my wordless behavior.

"I remember."

"Looks to me like he gave you a lot to think about." She gestured to my ring finger, holding up her own.

"There's nothing to think about. It's done."

June and Eliza exchanged a glance.

That morning, I was allowed to help with the dishes under the protests of June throughout the process. I had to find ways to occupy my time, didn't she understand that?

"What's that noise?" Before I could register the noise Eliza referred to, she answered her own question. "Get Porter, now June, like the devil is on your heels."

I dried off my hands while Eliza shuffled us both toward the back of the house, near Porter's office.

"You decide what to do here. No one is forcing you to do anything."

I opened my mouth to question her state of panic, but Porter entered the hallway before I could.

"Mother, June, stay in my office or the kitchen. Keep your ears open. Delilah, you come with me."

Grabbing my hand, he practically dragged me into the foyer and went about straightening his shirt and giving me a once-over.

"What is going on?" I found my voice and demanded an answer.

"Your parents are here. I suspected that they would show up. Your father hinted to the fact that the money I gave him might not be enough. I didn't think it would be this quick or I would've gotten you out of here."

I shuddered at his first sentence. The rest of his words blurred out.

"You gave him money? You bought me?"

This wasn't the time or the place to be angry, but damn it all to hell if I wasn't furious.

At the same time I understood and was grateful.

"Listen to me." Porter grabbed my shoulder with one hand and centered my chin with the other, his thumb and forefinger grabbing it. "This is your home. You are my wife. They cannot do anything to harm you here or I will show them the meaning of abuse. You do not belong to them anymore."

Finally coming to my senses, I grabbed his hands and implored him. "If you give them more money, they'll never stop."

A smile brought one side of his mouth up and the hand which was holding my chin left mine and cupped my left cheek—the one with the scar. "I know. Thank you."

I stared at him; his gray eyes held the same caress as the night before. For a tick of a second, his gaze moved down my lips. I tucked them in on instinct, uncomfortable with the insinuations my mind was making about his change.

But completely curious at the same time.

His thumb left my face and trailed a frustrating path along my already sensitive bottom lip.

"Another time, Delilah."

The sounds of horses snapped him out of our moment and into another mode. He held my hand and I trailed behind him while he surveyed the situation from a window.

"Your sisters and their husbands are here as well. Run and get my mother and June. Tell June to get tea ready and I want my mother with us to distract from any confrontation. Go!"

I did what I was told. It was the one thing I was good at.

"He says to get tea ready and Eliza, you're wanted with us. The whole family is here."

Eliza groaned. "Haven't they done enough damage? The gall of these people. Oh, sorry dear."

"Please don't apologize. I've said many a worse word about them inside my head."

We circumvented the niceties and went into the parlor and stoked the fire, ready for my wretched family's descent on what was otherwise a piece of heaven.

"Look at me, child."

My mother-in-law was dead serious.

"These people are visitors in your home — *your* home. They cannot make you feel like they did before without your permission. You're the best thing that's ever happened to my Porter. A mother knows these things."

She winked at me at the same time I heard the front door open. I fisted the bunching of fabric on my lap at the sound of my father's cantankerous cackle.

Porter led the pack into the sitting room. Eliza and I rose but I couldn't make myself meet their eyes.

"What a sight!" my mother heckled.

I kept my eyes firm on my husband. If it weren't for his wink I wouldn't have even remembered to breathe.

"Looks like the ugly chit hit the jackpot." I heard Adele whisper just quiet enough as not to be conceived as rude but loud enough to offend.

"We didn't expect your visit today. June will be in soon with the tea."

"You've got servants?" my father said, looking around the place like he was assessing the wealth of the wallpaper.

"We have a few — not many. I tend to do a lot of the work myself, though I didn't want Delilah to be bogged down with cooking or cleaning."

My left eyebrow pulsed toward my forehead in disbelief. He'd had the cook and the maid long before my arrival.

"Well, it must be nice to have people to help with the housework. My wrists and knuckles are always swollen from the amount of scrubbing it takes to keep my home in pristine condition."

I tried not to snicker the best way I knew how, by grinding my lips between my teeth.

Adele was sitting in the vicinity of Porter, and by vicinity, I meant four feet across the room, but with her complaint she jutted her hands out for visual proof of her work habits.

"I see that." But instead of her batting eyelashes reeling him in, he took a quick look from his seat and then reached over to take my hand in his.

I felt the stress drain from my body at once.

"This house must have many rooms. I'd love to see them."

My mother was a liar. She didn't want to see the rooms at all or make sure that I hadn't been kidnapped and taken to the dungeon of a snake lair.

She wanted to see what Porter was worth, assessing him by the stature of his property.

Porter and Eliza shared a look.

"Why don't we have some tea and then I'd love to show the place to you. I'm sure you want to make sure that the home your daughter is living in is safe and comfortable."

He'd nailed them to the ground with that one. It was becoming harder and harder for me to keep my composure but his hand squeezing mine was enough to bring me down.

"That would — that would be lovely."

Never in my life had I heard my mother use the term lovely.

June came in just in time and served everyone tea. I was served first and the looks that were shared between my sisters were vile enough to kill all the lightning bugs in the backyard.

I lifted my eyes to Porter in between sips and he'd taken to conversing with Elaine's husband about his manure business. After some minutes, my coy husband had even convinced the gangly man that he might be interested in investing in his business.

"How about that tour, Porter, dear? I don't like to be away from my home for very long at a time."

Porter never complained or showed one iota of frustration. I realized that what I was seeing was his diplomatic, business side. It was impeccable to be an audience to. He must've been able to rob people blind without them even knowing.

"Of course. Please, follow us."

I stayed seated, gluing my eyes to the tea cup before me. I must've looked like I was in a coma, eyes wide open.

"Delilah," he cooed at me. I looked up to see him holding out his hands, the party of tour goers waiting for him – and he waited on me. After placing my tea cup down, I took his hands. As I stood, he stooped to place a kiss along my brow and though the gesture put me in a bit of a trance, I heard the scoffing come from the direction of one of my sisters – probably the one that had done the slicing.

We conquered the upstairs first. Porter recited the same histories he had for me. I knew which bedroom he occupied after seeing one of the beds with fresh linens, not the ones I remembered seeing before.

"Which one of these is yours?"

I blushed, squeezing Porter's hand with an embarrassed fury. My sisters had about as much couth as a castrated pig.

"Our bedroom is the other wing, but I prefer to keep that private."

Adele choked on her drool. "The entire wing?"

"Yes. The entire wing. The rest of downstairs is my office, the library, and the drawing room. Those are not very interesting. Perhaps you'd like to see the outside."

My husband was smart. He was getting them out of the house under the premise of good manners.

"We actually should be going. Our horses seem to spook at night," Adele's husband said, plucking a stolen cookie from his pocket.

"Well, it was very nice having you over."

I thought the situation had been averted, until my father broke away from the pack.

"Porter, might I have a word with you, alone?"

"Sir, anything you say to me can be said in front of my wife. How can I help you?"

"Well, I'm not sure the sum you paid will cover the massive debt we are in because of the strain this one put on our finances after she went so long without being married."

I focused on my breaths. Inhaling and exhaling was the only thing I could count on. I didn't dare look at Porter's face. One look at him—deciding on shoving me back into the carriage they rode in on and demanding a refund for damaged goods—and I'd crackle into pieces and be blown like ashes with the wind.

My pulse bobbed in my temples and a bell rang in my ears.

Waiting—waiting on an almost stranger to decide my fate.

"You're right, Sir. I could sell everything I own and it wouldn't afford the blessing that is my wife. Leave the way you came. You won't get another cent from me. Get inside, Delilah."

My feet refused to budge.

He must've known that I'd turned to a statue because Porter, with a gentle hand, turned me around with his hands on my waist. I didn't remember getting inside or him sitting me by the fire. I must've been some proverbial ice queen. He was always rushing me to warmth.

"Tell me you're okay, sweetheart."

I could hear Porter's voice far away as if he called me from the surface while I was under a pool of water.

"I'm…"

It felt like someone else was moving my mouth for me.

Then I heard my new husband curse. I was lifted onto his lap and rocked in a comforting motion that not even my mother had ever attempted.

He was worried—the words that poured from his mouth dripped with syrupy concern.

"I'm okay," I was finally able to blurt.

"I would never let them hurt you."

I nodded and curled in closer to his embrace. His hold on me didn't falter. From my vantage point I focused on his stern jaw, the one that churned when he was upset about something. It was moving double time.

"Let me go," I said, wanting to stay in his arms, but also wanting to breathe.

"Of course." He set me on what he was now calling my chair.

Everything that I'd asked for was coming to fruition and I couldn't handle it.

"I'd like some coffee." The request surprised even me. I did want coffee. I thought the spurt of caffeine would shake the flood still washing over me. Porter sprang to action, calling for June while he took long strides toward the kitchen.

I also needed a second to myself to process my parents' visit.

"Here you go, dear." Eliza brought out a cup of coffee for me while Porter stayed behind, leaning against the threshold with his arms crossed over his chest.

I waited until Eliza left before turning to him. "Why are you so far away?"

"I thought you might want me to be."

"No. I never want you far away."

I meant it. The way he'd protected me against my parents in word and in contact would never cease to amaze me. I'd wished that we'd met another way, but if it took me a lifetime, I'd make sure the money Porter paid for me was well spent. He sat next to me while I took a few sips of the steaming coffee.

"Do you need something else?"

I shook my head. "No. I'm fine now. What were your plans for today?"

"It's your choice. Did they ruin our day?"

"No. I'm not that fragile, Porter. They shook me up, but I'm fine now — because of you."

He took my hands and held them tight. "How about a horse ride? Benjamin needs to be ridden daily, and I thought you might want to see the cabin on the outskirts of the property."

I nodded. "That sounds good. Let me grab a sweater."

I wasn't necessarily happy about riding on that beast again, but if my husband enjoyed it, I'd guessed that I should get used to the task. I grabbed a sweater I hadn't seen before from the wardrobe. It was longer than the other ones and had a tie around the middle. It was a fashion I'd never seen before but as long as it did its job, I really didn't care.

I'd certainly worn plenty of garments that barely did their job.

"I picked that one myself," Porter said from the bottom of the stairs. I'd been too busy making my hair cover the side of my face to realize he was waiting for me.

"Thank you — again."

"Stop thanking me."

"Stop thanking you and stop saying sorry."

I was kidding but my remark caused his face to drop in sadness.

"I wasn't trying to boss you around. I just didn't want you to feel obligated to apologize for anything. And isn't part of the fun of being a husband getting to buy things for his wife?"

I'd never seen my father have such fun.

"To each his own, I suppose. But when do I get to give you something?"

I'd finally reached the stairs when his hand reached mine. "The things you give me cannot be bought with money, Delilah."

I hadn't realized I'd given him anything but a hole in his pockets and a headache.

"Let's go before it gets too late. It's already early afternoon."

My family's tour of the house must've taken longer than I assumed. Then again, I was mostly in a trance the entire time, hoping one of them didn't try to rustle the curtains under their skirts or produce a knife from one of their purses and try to finish what they'd started on my face — or worse, try to hurt Porter.

We walked out to the stables. When the worn building came into view, I remembered Rebel and his haunting stare.

His words had slithered over me like an invisible cobweb. I contained a shiver, but just barely.

"Benjamin doesn't get ridden very much. He's fickle and won't let anyone else ride him."

He walked into the barns and Benjamin whinnied from the back, letting Porter know he'd been waiting.

"Can you do me a favor? Take this while I saddle him up."

I took the bag from him. I hadn't even noticed he was carrying a bag before. I watched as he sweet-talked Benjamin into leaving the stall and gave him a full brushing before saddling the tallest horse I'd ever seen.

Chapter Eight

On the ride to the cabin, my insides were still shaking from the confrontation with her father. Until the words left my mouth, I hadn't really planned anything for the day, other than riding Benjamin. Rebel wasn't in the barn which meant he'd finished his jobs for the day and had flown to his home as soon as possible. He'd never done anything other than the bare minimum.

It was a selfish thing I was doing, bringing her to the cabin. My mother called it the honeymoon cabin. She and my father used to go out there for weekends, leaving me with June, who was the nanny and the cook at the time.

I got onto the horse first, after securing the bag, and then reached for Delilah. But this time, she sat in front of me instead of behind me. I placed her sideways so that her modesty wouldn't be compromised. It was important to her, I could tell. I still wasn't sure of her state after the morning's events. She seemed jumpy and frail. The ride would be good for both of us.

"They've hated me all of my life," she whispered halfway through our journey.

"Why?"

"I'm not sure. I did everything I was told. I got good marks in school. I can't cook a thing, Porter. I wouldn't know how to make biscuits if someone glued the instructions to my face."

She was funny. I bet no one else knew that about her. She hadn't mentioned any friends. My stomach soured at the fleeting thought of another man who may have held her heart, even as a friend.

"June won't allow you to cook, anyway. The only thing Mother is allowed to do is make tea."

She crooked her neck in my direction. Her body moved with the jerk, causing me to tighten my grip at her waist.

"Then why did you ask me if I could cook? I nearly fainted when you asked that."

I shrugged. "I thought it was what I was supposed to ask. All of my breath was lost when you came down the stairs."

"I bet it was."

"Hey, none of that." I kissed her temple. I'd done it like it was second nature to me. "Sorry. It was—I didn't think."

A tear streamed down her face—just one. "It's not an imposition, Porter. Trust me."

I made a mental note of her acceptance of affection. I had made sure not to invade her space, but it seemed she didn't mind.

"Why did you think they hated you?"

"It wasn't just me. They hated themselves. They treated their home like trash. They didn't bathe regularly. They hated everything around them—and at the same time criticized those who didn't live up to their high standards. I don't know why they hated me. It was enough to make them attempt to ruin me or kill me, I don't know which. We didn't speak of it."

"Did you go to the doctor? Didn't they ask you how it happened?"

"I never went to the doctor. I cleaned it myself, after I had woken up. Mrs. Calhoun gave me some salve to put on it, but it didn't stop the pain."

"I'm glad I didn't know that before they came this morning."

"Why?"

I pushed a chunk of hair from her face. "Because they would've never been allowed in our home."

Her eyes cast downward, taking my answer into consideration. The longer we rode, the closer she snuggled to me. There was no doubt that Delilah had gotten under my skin just by being who she was, but when she was this close, smelling like the calendula flowers that used to grow in the beds outside, it was nearly impossible not to take her lips.

We got to the cabin in less than an hour. It hadn't been kept up. That was one of the reasons I wanted Delilah to come out with me. Since this cabin would now be ours, I wanted her to be in charge of redoing it—if she wanted to.

"This is it." I dismounted the horse and reached for Delilah. She took my arms willingly.

"It's a lovely little cottage."

It could've been a cottage. That was my mother's initial intention. Father turned it into more of a hunting cabin. Even when they came out here, mother complained to June that it was used more as a smelly fish keeper than a romantic getaway.

I hoped it would be different for us.

"It needs a makeover. We could paint it any color you like, make it look more like a cottage."

She pointed to herself and I laughed.

"Yes. You. The cabin is ours after all."

A beaming smile took over her face. She turned to me and then back to the cabin. I thought maybe she'd run to me.

"Can we go in?"

"Of course"

I pulled the skeleton key from my pocket and unlocked the door carefully. I wasn't sure what awaited us, so I took my time, allowing a fair warning for any creatures that had made their home here. It was as I remembered it from sneaking here as a child. It was rustic to say the least. The walls boasted of my father's kills and the curtains looked more like a camouflaged man's attire than a woman's retreat.

"This is it."

She said nothing.

"I know. It's not the cottage you were thinking."

Her blank face was frustrating.

"Say something. I swear, anything you have to say—I won't take offense."

After giving the place a once over through her icy eyes, she said. "It stinks."

"Like fish."

"Like rotten crawfish and moldy potatoes."

I sighed and sat down in a chair that openly protested my weight.

"Can we start by taking down the camouflage? I feel like I'm being hunted."

With the cabin stripped of everything except the furniture, I stepped back and watched Delilah take the last blanket out and pile it up with the rest. Despite her father's insistence that she was lazy, she'd worked harder than I had during the day.

I worked on sweeping out the inside. It was all that was left to be done. For a place that never got used, it was dingy and dusty as if it got used every day.

A sound stilled my movements. I dropped the broom and ran toward the scream as fast as my legs would carry me. I didn't hear anything else. Panic struck me.

"Delilah!"

Nothing. Not even the sounds of the land around me gave any clues.

I continued walking, faster and faster in the direction I thought the cry for help had come from. If something had happened to her already, I wouldn't be able to handle it.

A giggle in front of me carried on the wind. There was no child around, but it echoed around me, calling me forward. That's when I saw Delilah crawling on her hands and knees away from the small pond that my father used to fish in. Terror was written all over her face.

"Delilah!"

Her eyes widened and that's when I realized. She wasn't just getting away from whatever had frightened her—she was getting away from me.

"I'm not going to hurt you. Please!"

She stopped and countless times looked between me and the water. No one had been to this place to fish in a while, but I couldn't imagine anything that would scare her to this degree.

I approached her as slowly as I was able to. Step by step she lost her heaving breaths and the fear trickled out of her eyes.

"Can I..."

She didn't let me finish, choosing instead to vault herself up from her sitting position and nearly tackled me. For a tiny thing, she hung on for dear life.

I was useless against her cries.

Chapter Nine

There was no way in Hades that I'd imagined it, yet as I recalled the event that froze my heart and sent the terror of murder through my veins, the vision refused to be disputed.

I'd seen the girl — in the water.

Her white dress remained and she'd stayed the age of the plump toddler, sweet-faced, with rounded cheeks and baby knuckles.

Until the vision was no longer a vision.

Toddler transformed into woman, reaching out from the depths with arms as cold and clammy as a dead fish. She reached for my throat. And murder lay in her eyes.

Her battle cry still blasted in my ears.

Hands were felt on my neck as real as Porter's as he attempted to contain my shudders.

I'd gone over to the pond just to rinse my hands of the dust that clung to my palms. Never did I image what awaited me beneath the truth of the surface.

No, no, I was wrong.

I began to excuse the floating image at once recalling my shot nerves from the morning's drama.

That must've been it.

My imagination had gotten away from me, fueled by the haunting books from the time spent reading the day before.

It was all a ruse of my wild mind.

"What happened?"

"I—I thought I saw something. I'm just overtired and hungry."

That was the general excuse for everything in this place—I knew it would go over.

"Are you sure? Come, let's get away from the water."

Porter was about as happy as me to still be in visual distance of the pond. We walked back to the cabin, me still under the protection of his arm, though it did nothing to lessen my quaking.

"We are going to go home and you are going to eat and get some rest. I won't take no for an answer."

Words carried on the wind as he rushed me home. I felt like an incapable twit, being carried home and fed and rested. I'd gone from being everyone's unpaid servant to being tip-toed around like a pampered princess.

I didn't like it one bit.

It wasn't so bad, though.

It was nice to be looked after.

I rolled my eyes at my constant internal arguing. Any girl would give a hand or even an organ to be treated half as well as Porter was treating me.

Yet, I complained.

The cypress trees' limbs were lower near his home. Their leaves bowed in sadness. Even the grass bowed down to the side a little, the surrounding doom too much for them to bear.

We got to the house and the twit was handed off to Eliza while Porter made his excuses of getting Benjamin back to the stalls.

"I'm fine." I thrust myself out of Eliza's hold and forwent the former suggestion that I eat and sit in front of the fire like a kept woman. The stairs were taken two at a time while I made my way to the bedroom and shut the door behind me. I needed a bath and some time alone. I was sure that a few minutes of normalcy would cure me—and being by myself was as normal as it got for me.

I turned on the water, as hot as I could take it, and stared down into the clear abyss, daring the vision to show itself. Of course it didn't. It was a farce, after all.

My clothes hit the floor just seconds before my toe dipped into the water, testing it for heat. It was the hottest water I'd known. Even warming water over the wood stove didn't bring water to this temperature.

The rhythm of the drips coming from the faucet became my heartbeat. I had to get ahold of myself. I'd never had Porter before, but in the span of three days, I'd become dependent on his presence. It was imperative that I stop seeking him for everything — after all, he'd be gone a good deal of the time.

I sighed, making ripples in the water underneath my chin. It was too late. Already, I missed him and I'd been in the bath less than a half hour.

Closing my eyes, all I could see was those savage eyes — black to my blue. She'd been dressed in white again and in the seconds she reached for me, morphed from a child to a woman — a woman with the very devil in her eyes.

I slowed my breaths and made myself listen for the drips from the faucet again.

Maybe the events of my life were just catching up with me — just waiting in the wings for a peaceful pause to come out and rehash themselves.

Porter had looked as terrified as I felt.

He was just protecting his investment, right?

A knock at the bathroom door jarred me. I knew he'd be concerned, but had no idea he'd go so far as to come into the bathroom.

"I'm in the bath."

I'd purposefully said it quietly so I could blame the door for any misunderstanding.

"I know, but I have to make sure you're okay."

"I'm fine."

There was a clunk on the door. The tips of his shoes were visible underneath it. It was his head. He'd thumped it on the door in exhaustion of my antics.

Three days — that must've been a record for me.

"You have to cover your eyes."

"I promise."

What in the heck was I thinking?

He opened the door and came in, head down and eyes covered by his hands. I drew my knees up to my chest in an effort to be a little modest, despite the circumstances. Porter felt for the edge of the porcelain and then laid on the tiled floor next to the tub. I leaned over the edge, just to reveal my face and dripped water on his. He squinted and turned his face as the droplets rained havoc on him.

"Hey, you're taking the bath, not me."

I bit my lip and rolled my eyes. "So, I'm okay. You can see it."

"What happened out there?"

I leaned my face against the side of the tub where it was cool, trying to hide my blush.

"I went to the pond because my hands were full of dust. I washed them in the water and then I heard a bubbling—a noise in the water as though a fish had surfaced."

He rose to rest on his elbows, his face was inches from mine. His gray eyes were manic, irises searching, waiting for the next detail.

"That's when I saw her, the little girl."

"Marie."

"Yes. She was a child in the water. I panicked and did the first thing I thought of. I reached for her and she reached back."

Having heard the insane words aloud made me deflate and I flopped back into the bath, splashing him again.

"Sorry." He got up and got a towel, never breaking our deal. He laid back down next to me, this time his fingers playing with the tips of my pruned ones hanging like a fern over the edge of the tub.

"It's fine. Tell me the rest."

"When she reached for me, she changed a bit—got older. I swear I felt her hands around my neck. Her eyes—I've never seen anything so grim—so onerous."

He sat up quickly, so much so that I didn't have time to be upset. If I thought his eyes were penetrating before, when they met mine in sheer panic, it felt like a physical invasion.

"She touched you?"

A tear slipped from my eye. I couldn't look at him. If there was an inkling of disbelief in his voice, I wouldn't be able to bear it.

I tried to look out of the windows to soothe myself, but the steam from the bath had thrown a cloudy film over the stained glass windows that surrounded the cove in which the bathtub kept its home.

His hand touched a hair that stuck out from the bun I'd piled my hair into. He tucked several wisps behind my ear, the ear next to the scar. Everything on my body was in relation to the scars. Prickles rose on my neck, his breaths across my skin making every cell buzz. The temperature of the water was nothing compared to the fire blazing through my veins. Porter was so close.

"We decided no secrets, love."

I shivered at the use of that word. Never had I been the recipient of that word.

"She tried to strangle me."

I heard the thump of his forehead on the tub. He rubbed my shoulder, kneading the muscles there, but I swore I could feel him everywhere.

"Can I see them?"

Must every conversation turn to those blasted cuts?

"Porter." His name lodged in my throat, so many unbidden emotions tangled with it.

"I'd never hurt you. You know that, don't you?"

I turned my head to see him. His face showed me every emotion, even when he refused to speak. There was undaunted truth in his determined mouth. He held his breath, waiting on my answer.

I wanted to show him everything that was me. Lay it out on a table of freedom and let him pick through the pieces.

"I trust you."

The three most telling words I'd ever muttered.

"Move up a little. I don't want to see anything you don't want me to. I am a gentleman after all."

As if I didn't know.

I scooted up in the now tepid water, it sloshed along the sides of my torso. I shook in place, holding my arms around my knees, a foiled attempt at containing the shivering from nothing other than my husband's proximity to a body and a soul untouched.

But craving it with an intensity that bordered on carnal.

I sucked in a breath through clenched teeth when his fingers made their first contact with my other shoulder. My sisters hadn't been satisfied with marring my face. When I turned to run after waking up from the attack, they cut into my back like one skins and guts a swine.

"You never saw a doctor? These are deep."

"No, they didn't take me and I was in no condition to take myself. After a week or so, I got up one morning, got dressed, and went about like nothing had happened."

I couldn't hear the dripping anymore. The drumming of my heart in my temples overrode everything else. His hand was now splayed against the small of my back. There were no scars there.

"You're so soft. I knew you would be."

"You've touched me before, Porter."

His answer came in the form of a breathless whisper in my ear. "Not like this. Not nearly enough. There are times in the day when you are next to me and yet you feel so far away. I don't know how I'm going to cope when I have to go out on business."

Porter's hand continued to run a haughty path up and down my back and it sounded in my core as though he stroked an artery, connected to every part of me, sending life to every cell.

"Thank you for trusting me." I nearly whimpered at the loss of his touch when he removed his hand. "I don't know what to make of what you saw. I'm not saying you didn't see it, but I just don't know what it could be."

He was lying. The hitch of his voice told me that there was, in fact, some farce in his words. My heart and my head were at war and so were his.

"I think I'm hungry."

I was hungry, but I'd intended to ignore the sensation.

"You're just in time for supper. Would you rather take it in here? I'll bring it here. You don't even have to see anyone else if you don't want to."

"Will you join me? I've found that I don't like to eat alone."

"You read my mind. I'll give you time to get dressed."

He left the room and shut the door behind him. I smiled at myself in the mirror like a girl who'd just gotten her first kiss. My cheeks flushed with newfound strength.

I chose a simple white blouse and a navy skirt, forgoing the boots or the stockings. I hated stockings anyway. Looking in the mirror, I rushed to brush through my hair and pinned it into a suitable bun. Long gone was the sham of trying to cover up my scar with my hair. There were no longer any scars that I could keep from him.

The room was cold and the beginnings of a night thunderstorm brewed outside. The clouds never lied.

"I brought a little of everything." Porter scared the cold right out of my bones. I danced an embarrassing display of fear mixed with tap. "I swear I didn't marry you to give you a heart attack."

I fisted my shirt at my chest. "It's fine. I'm just jumpy. Too much coffee. I don't think I'll truly ever understand why you married me." The words tumbled from my brain straight out of my mouth. My filter had dissolved since marrying Porter.

"Do you want me to tell you why?"

"I don't mean to sound ungrateful."

"You're anything but ungrateful. Let's eat and I'll tell you about it."

He placed the tray full of savory gumbo and bread on the circular table that sat in the corner of the room. We both ate half a bowl before he began.

"I'd gone into town to handle a bad loan. It was in the alleys behind The Plots. I heard some ruckus. At first, I thought it was a person selling newspapers, so I ignored it."

"My father."

"Yes." He reached over and grabbed my hand. I supposed he was anchoring me in case the rest of the story was as horrid as I'd imagined. "He was — he was selling you off like a piece of meat, Delilah. The men around him were making lewd jokes and cackling. I didn't even know you — hadn't even seen you — but something made me want to…"

"Save me."

"Yes. Whoever you were, I wanted to get you away from that horrid man. I'd even planned to come to your home and propose and then set you loose with enough money to get you by for a while."

My chest moved up and down with humiliating force with every word. "I can't listen to any more." I wrenched my hand from his and walked over to the window, the rain knocking on the panes, wanting a way in.

"Delilah, you have to listen, love. Please, listen to me. I need you to know."

His chin rested upon the top of my head, bobbing with every sentiment. His chest rumbled against my shoulders as he spoke. It was as though he'd taken me into every concave of his stature. I felt secure.

"I'm listening."

"I went to your home that day as a man wanting to set a captive free. Anyone could see that your father was desperate, and I couldn't imagine a young woman in the hands of the rest of those miscreants."

Porter slid his hands down my arms, ending by threading his fingers through mine. This was not the story I'd imagined. It was far worse. After a few moments of silence, I nodded just to let him know that he could continue.

"I went into your home and..."

I turned my head a bit. "Be honest, Porter. You can't say anything to offend me. I lived there."

"So true." He chuckled and kissed my head. "It was filthy. It stank. I instantly pitied anyone whose family chose to live like that. Then you came down the stairs. Your mother was holding a candle. Its light reflected on your eyes just so—I thought I was hallucinating. Then I saw the scar and the way your father talked about you. You were so thin—so frail. Yet their words didn't seem to have any effect on you. I wanted you for my own. I was selfish. I should've let you go. I know I'm not the kind of man you probably wanted."

I turned and gripped his waist with my face pressed against his chest. "I can't imagine anyone else I'd want."

He placed his finger beneath my chin and tipped my face upward. "There's no pity anymore, Delilah. It has been replaced by love."

I saw the look in his eyes. Even if a girl has never been kissed, the look in a man's eyes when his mind is set on kissing you is inherent, like it's coded into our brains from birth. It was the look on Porter's face.

There were no defenses in my arsenal to stop him—and I had no want to.

"Can I kiss you, wife?"

"Yes."

The first touch of his mouth was warm. His lips were softer than I'd expected, warmer than a thousand sunrises. Bristling heat moved across my face and down my neck with every stroke of my lips against his. My body swayed into his and he caught me without ever breaking our connection.

It was one thing to hear that someone loved you, but to feel it in their embrace was another altogether.

It was a kiss that wove two people together.

I was no judge of a kiss—but there were no other competitors next to Porter.

"I've been waiting to do that forever."

Smiling, I swatted his shoulder. "We've been married less than a week."

"If I'd known it would be like that, I wouldn't have waited less than a minute."

I sighed and fell against him again in awe.

How did I get so lucky?

"Do you want to have dessert downstairs? My mother is a little worried about you."

"Sure. She's very kind to me. Like a real mother."

He picked up the tray with our unfinished dinner and turned. "You're happy here?"

"Yes. Of course I am. Why wouldn't I be?"

Chapter Ten

I paced the office in the middle of the night, plowing through the events of the past few days. I didn't know what to make of it.

Yes, Marie was a bothersome girl when she was alive.

But in death, she hadn't ever bothered me, only appearing here and there in awkward spaces — always silent.

Delilah had been through so much in her life. She knew the truth of things and wasn't one of these women who created drama out of boredom.

If she said she saw something in the water, then she did.

I picked up a letter that must've come in during the day. There was an issue at one of the banks I owned and my presence was mandatory. I had to leave the day after next.

Instead of wanting to run from a woman like I did Marie, I wanted to cling to Delilah.

I sat down and rested my head in my hands. I'd tried to love Marie, I had.

It wasn't enough in the end. That's why she haunted me.

Ultimately, my lack of love had been her demise.

"Good morning." Delilah stuck her head around the corner into my office. "Why the face?"

"It's the only one I have."

I sighed. "You know what I mean. Is something the matter?"

A bell rang in the distance. It was June letting everyone know that breakfast was ready.

"Why don't you go eat breakfast and then we will talk."

She didn't look pleased with my suggestion.

"Why don't you come sit with us while we eat? It will do you good to get out of this office. You've been here all night."

"Come here, Delilah." She walked over, the swish of her skirt the only thing I could hear. When she reached the desk, she paused. "Sit here in front of me. I want to see you."

She ran her fingers down her nose in that gesture I'd come to love as much as her. She was showing her shyness.

"Can I ask you a question?"

"Of course."

"I have to know something. Have you kissed another man before?"

Her whole body tensed. Her gaze darted around the room to anything other than my face.

"Once, a boy kissed me on the playground. I was five."

I laughed and rested my weary head on her legs, wrapping my arms around them. She ran her hands through my hair and I thought if there was a heaven, it was there under the care of my wife.

"I've never been kissed like that. Not ever. Was—was it okay?"

"It was perfect."

"Then why did you need to know?"

I shrugged and confessed, "For my own well-being—nothing more."

"Come eat with me. You look so tired."

"If you insist."

She was right. The laughter and boasting at my table was more fun than I'd had in a while, other than delighting in my new wife. I actually ate breakfast for the first time in a long time until I remembered that I had to break my promise to stay with Delilah for a week.

"Can we talk for a moment?" I asked her with my hand on her elbow.

"Yes. Can we go outside?"

"Sure."

We walked outside to the porch, choosing rocking chairs next to each other. I reveled in the moment for a second, happy that finally someone was by my side.

"I have to leave tomorrow. Just for a day."

I reached for her hand.

"I understand. You'll be back tomorrow night?"

"I hope so. I will do my best."

Delilah grew quiet beside me. I had disappointed her again. Everything she'd been through and I was abandoning her.

At the same time, I had to support her. She deserved this life — to be spoiled.

Out of nowhere she laughed a little and then covered her mouth.

"What is funny?"

"Your mother mentioned me learning to embroider like she does. I tried once. I sewed my skirt to the fabric I was working on. I was so proud of that little daisy until I realized it was sewn to me. That was my first and last lesson in embroidering."

I wonder if she'd shared that story with anyone before. I doubted it.

"You could always help me." My voice intonated as though I'd asked a question.

"You'd let me?"

"Of course. We'll look over everything later. It will keep you busy that way you won't have time to pine after me the entire day."

I froze as Delilah turned on me, the look in her eyes burned my skin. "I don't think anyone or anything could keep me from pining for you all day. I may as well just sleep the day through to save myself the torture."

My breath was still held. It was a bold declaration, and so out of character.

And then she broke out in a fit of laughter.

"You were joking? That's fine. I see how you feel." I crossed my arms and looked in the opposite direction, willing my mouth not to smile.

"Oh, I'm sorry, Porter. I was just kidding." She sighed and I let her stew a minute before turning to her with a broad smile on my face.

"You are horrible, Porter Jeansonne!"

"I didn't know you were capable of such blatant sarcasm, Mrs. Jeansonne. Shame on you."

She sobered, but stayed smiling, biting her lip. "I didn't either."

Chapter Eleven

Most of the day came and went in a blur. Porter's office was a mess. I'd straightened everything and organized some of his things. There was a wooden box stuffed into his drawer. It was so ornately designed that I removed it and placed it on his bookshelf, replacing the ghastly unshuffled papers. He had pens scattered in every cranny. For a man that had it all together, he was completely unorganized.

By the afternoon, I was tired of being cooped up. June and Eliza took a trip to town to get groceries and other things for the house and I'd opted to stay home. I didn't want to run into my family without Porter.

I grabbed my long coat and went out toward the back. The sun threatened to come over the trees, but like any other day, it shied away from this place. Like there was an invisible border over Jeansonne Manor that halted its rise in the sky.

Drawing in a deep breath, I tromped down the stairs. My shoes squished into the damp grass from the prior day's rain, but I was determined to get some fresh air. Jeansonne Manor sat in the middle of the swamp, like its own island. There was a bridge that led from the land to the road to the town. Porter had told me there was another bridge on the back of the property that led to the outside cities.

I followed the path of rocks to the pond and crept up on it, cautious of what lay beneath the still water. I hadn't seen or heard anything since the day at the pond. I'd prayed day and night that the incident was the end of whatever torment the woman had to dole out.

"This is where she died." A gravelly voice interrupted my stare. To my left was Rebel, dressed in pants and a grimy shirt with suspenders over it. His boots were worn over his pants and they were a tell-tale sign of his employment. He was too close to me. I could feel the heat of his body radiating off of him in waves.

"Who?"

He chuckled; the sound of it twisted my gut. I squirmed in place, off-put by his crassness.

"What a shame. A new wife that knows nothing about the manor she is mistress over. You've a lot to learn. I'm sure Porter has been teaching you many things."

I was tangled in Rebel's web. Porter had secrets. Rebel knew what they were. But the atmosphere soured when he was around. I didn't wish to spend one more minute around him.

Anger consumed me at the audacity of this man. He claimed to know things but taunted me with them.

"Just tell me who died here."

He shoved a hand into his shirt where he fondled something that hung around his neck. Rocking back and forth on his heels, he continued to ignore me.

"Delilah? Oh, there you are child. Come inside, we've got things to unpack."

Eliza called to me from the house but I hadn't gotten any information out of the man who made my skin crawl.

"Excuse me," I said, wondering why I wasted manners on someone who obviously had none.

"Delilah, one thing."

I turned with one fist pressed on my hip.

"Ask Porter about Marie."

With a roll of my eyes, I stalked into the house, unfazed by his attempted meddling.

I helped June and Eliza put the groceries away. I didn't understand the gall of that man—Rebel-- butting into my business when all I'd wanted to do was stare blankly at the land and take a walk.

He was always around when Porter wasn't.

When I was a child, I cried at all the time I'd had by myself with no one to confide in and no one to play with. And now as an adult, married and thrust into a life that would make anyone else faint with bliss — all I wanted in the world was a moment of peace.

Porter knew about the ghost. He knew what she'd done to me. She'd attacked me. If I'd let her, I would bet she would've dragged me down in the water with her.

"Delilah, maybe you should go rest or have some tea."

I ticked my eyes over to Eliza. "Why?"

"Because we need those carrots."

I'd been wringing the carrots together like they were a sopping washcloth. The poor things were nearly shredded.

"I'm sorry. I'm a little high strung today. I'm going to the library. Maybe a book would calm me down."

They looked on me like I was a stranded puppy.

I may have been stranded, but I wasn't pathetic.

Clumsily, I slid down to the floor in the library after shutting the door behind me. Concentrating on my breaths, I made an attempt at calming down. The library was quite possibly the most beautiful room in the house. It even beat the bedroom. There were cypress shelves that ran floor to ceiling. Even the floors beneath me were worn and weathered cypress. The whole room smelled like river water and book pages. I wanted to bottle it.

I took to wringing my hands instead of the poor carrots.

"This is ridiculous." I said aloud.

I grabbed a book from behind me, not even looking at the title and opened it to the middle and decided to read the first passage, vowing to take the sentence as an omen.

"Every heart is haunted."

I had to ask Porter about Marie. Maybe if I knew the story, I would be better equipped to handle her if she showed up again.

Then again, knowledge didn't exactly serve as a shield for strangulation.

He asked that we have no secrets.

I trusted Porter.

I had to tell him.

Chapter Twelve

Benjamin was more cautious than usual as we crossed the bridge at the back of the property and even attempted not to make the last steps onto our land.

"Benjamin, come on boy. We are home."

He didn't want to move on, but he obeyed anyway. I passed by the cabin and found its door wide open along with the windows. Looking around the area, no one was near, but the whole thing felt like one of those wormy Rebel tricks.

I decided to leave the issue for later, wanting more than anything to get back to Delilah. The sun wasn't my friend, fading more and more as I rode home. The land was mushy and waterlogged as we rode through it slowly. Benjamin didn't like the mud and he faltered more than once. By the time we reached the house, the sun had completely failed me, hiding now behind the moon.

The meeting at my office hadn't gone as long as I'd thought, so I made it a point to go to the bookstore and get

Delilah more books. I intended to replace the dull ones on accounting and business with books for her, little by little.

I wanted her to feel like this was her home too.

It was her home.

After settling Benjamin into the stalls, I assessed the place. There was barely enough feed for the rest of the week and the conditions were deplorable at best. Rebel, again, wasn't working up to snuff.

I cleaned up Benjamin's stall myself and gave him enough food and water to last until I could get ahold of Rebel. His father was the same, never working up to our expectations.

Generations ago, my great-great-grandfather's life was saved by a member of Rebel's family. In a fit of shock, my ancestor promised Rebel's family that they would always have a job at our estate if they needed one.

They had no idea that Rebel would one day come along.

After chucking my boots off on the front steps, I went into the house and wiped my forehead. There was sweat. Smiling to myself, I knew the reason for the anxiety. I was nervous as a school boy to see Delilah.

I'd been laughed at in the meeting for drifting into thought. The men in the room knew how it was to be in the honeymoon phase of a marriage. They'd razzed me for a half an hour before deciding they didn't need me much after all, just my signature.

I had to see her. Even if she was asleep and unaware of my presence.

I twisted the knob to the bedroom as quietly as I could, making sure to push the door with a jerk to avoid the squeak.

Holding my breath, I approached the bed. The curtains around it were loose and it was freezing in the room. Willing my heartbeat to slow, I pulled one of the curtains open.

The bed was empty.

Perplexed, I stalked to the bathroom and searched the bathroom and in the closets for good measure. She wasn't anywhere to be found.

I tromped downstairs and searched the usual places along with my library. There were several books on the chair and a blanket was draped over the chair. She'd been there at some point.

The more I look and didn't find her, the more worried I became.

With so many unknowns about the things that had happened to her, my worst fears played in a horrific slideshow in my mind.

I went to the other end of the house and knocked on my mother's bedroom. She snored like a bear and it took a few raps before she finally woke up and answered.

"Porter. What's the matter? It's the middle of the night."

"I can't find Delilah. She's not in bed and I've looked everywhere."

She tied the sash of her robe around her waist, cinching it tight. "After supper, she said she was going to bed. She had a heck of a day. The sadness was written clear across her face."

"Can you help me look?"

"Of course."

We scrambled through the house, June eventually joining us. We'd made enough commotion in the house to wake the dead. Though from the last week's events, the dead were already alive and well. Room by room we checked.

"I'll get my coat and start outside," I barked at my mother who agreed.

I'd just reached for my boots when I heard June talking behind me. "She's in your room, Porter. Bless her heart."

I backtracked, going back upstairs without a second look to June or my mother. I had heard her giggle as I passed, but I no longer cared.

If a man was desperate about anything, it should be getting to his wife.

And that's all I wanted.

The door to my room was shut. In my search, I'd overlooked it, thinking that she'd never go in there. There was no reason to. I was wrong.

As I opened the door, I was hit with a vision from a dream. Delilah was laying on her side, facing the door, her arms wrapped around my pillow for dear life. I let out a breath I'd been holding since I'd seen her bed empty and closed the door behind me.

The girl who not long ago was a withered flower with torn petals and too many thorns had come back to life. In just a week's time she had changed into a beauty among women. Her cheeks had filled out a bit. Though she was covered with a blanket, I could see the change in her shape. What once was a thinning body that mirrored a skeleton more than a lady was now taking the shape of a vixen. Her raven hair spilled onto the white pillow below her head like ink blotted on paper.

And I knew behind those peaceful eyelids were a pair of iridescent blue eyes that sunk me with every blink.

I grabbed my night clothes and intended to sneak out of the room when a voice so tender and true stopped me cold. "Porter?"

"It's late, love. I'm going to sleep in another room. Everything is fine."

"Don't leave me." Those three words, whispered in the darkness, ended any chances I had of keeping my promise of leaving her alone intact.

I sat on the edge of the bed and held her hand.

Please don't be enough. Please want more from me. Please want me to hold you.

"Are you okay?"

She replaced the pillow in its spot and leaned on her elbow, scooting closer to me. "I am now."

"Did something happen?"

"No. I—I missed you terribly."

She looked down as if missing me was something to be ashamed of.

"I did too—so much."

"Can you stay with me tonight?"

I hadn't realized how much I'd needed to hear those words until she'd spoken them. They went straight to my heart. Not because of the promise of something more, but her simple request of my presence was enough.

"Of course. Let me go change into my pajamas."

After I'd changed into my pajama pants, I sat down on the bed again. I wanted to be sure she wanted me with her.

"Are you sure?"

"I am."

Moving the covers, I laid next to her close enough to feel her warmth but far enough away to give her space.

"How was your trip?"

Her hand found mine under the blanket. I turned to face her and mimicked her pose, resting on my elbow.

"It was fine. I brought you something."

"You've got to stop this, Porter. I don't want things."

Reaching out to touch her hair, I pressed the issue. "What do you want?"

"I want joy and peace."

"You don't have that?"

"I'm getting there." She released my hand and touched my chest. "What do *you* want, Porter?"

"I just want your love."

She gasped and a lone tear dropped from the cliff of her eye. "You have it."

My heart beat double-time. It was so loud, I was sure everyone in the house could hear it pounding. We lay in silence for a few moments, drinking each other in by the light of the bayou moon.

I yawned and Delilah giggled. "Let's go to sleep."

"It's going to be a task with you over there."

She moved closer, lining her body up flush with mine and then rested her cheek on my chest. "Sleep, Porter."

"Goodnight, Delilah."

I woke but kept my eyes shut. The absence of her feather weight and delicate smell was noticed immediately. I shot up to a sitting position only to have my fear quelled by the sight of Delilah sitting by the window.

"Good morning."

"Good morning to you. It's late, but you looked so tired. I didn't want to wake you."

"Come here."

She got up, adjusting the robe to assure her modesty and then climbed back into bed, kneeling beside me. Her hair was long and straight. The ends of it tickled my stomach.

"I didn't want to leave the room. I'm afraid of your mother seeing me here."

"She already knows, Delilah. Besides, we're married. It's okay to sleep with your husband."

Her hands flew to her face and she leaned over to lay across my chest. "That's the first time you've called yourself my husband."

"If it makes you blush and throw yourself at me, then I'll have to say it more often."

"Porter!" She moved, nudging me in jest. Her hair was all around me, over my stomach, on my sides, and spilling like water over her shoulders.

I didn't think I'd known true happiness until that moment, having her so close.

Who knew so much could change with one night spent next to someone you loved.

"Anyway, it was my mother who found you here. We'd been looking for...it felt like for hours and then she found you. I was about to go insane with worry."

Slowly she turned. She ran her hands through my hair and down the scruff I'd grown from being away until the morning. "One time when I was about fourteen, I decided to run away. My mom had blamed me for something—I don't even remember what. So, I ran out and to the land by the small pond at the north of the village. Do you know which one I'm talking about?"

"Sable's pond." I added and sat up so that I could see her better.

"I went there and spent two nights without a fire. I don't know how to build a fire. My parents didn't want me handling the firewood. They were afraid I was going to throw them into it or something. After two nights of freezing almost to death, I went home. My mother accused me of trying to get a job at The Plots. She went on and on for months about how she didn't blame them for turning down someone like me." Her voice waivered with the last word. She'd hidden the pain of how her parents treated her for too long with no one to give it to. I would take it all from her — take it upon myself to ease her burden.

"They're not welcome in our home. I know they are your parents and I allowed one visit to tamper down any rumors flying around, but hearing what they put you through—I won't tolerate them in our home. I won't give them a chance to hurt you again. And for the record, you are the most beautiful woman I've ever seen. I swear you grow more and more alluring by the day."

Delilah ticked her eyes to the side of the bed. It would take a lifetime to undue her parents' abuse. I was happy to be tasked with the responsibility.

"Thank you. I'd better go get dressed. We should at least try to make it down for breakfast."

"We should."

She rose from the bed and opened the door, looking left and right as though she were about to cross the street.

"Are you going to do that every morning?" I poked fun at her anxiety.

"Who says this will be a recurring event?"

I walked over to her and pulled her back against me while shutting the door.

"Are you saying you didn't like sleeping next to me?"

Her breathing became labored. I placed my mouth next to her ear. "Delilah, is that what you're saying?"

"No."

"Good. Hurry up and get to breakfast."

I hadn't let her go and didn't release her when she made a move to leave.

"Porter."

"You'd leave me without a kiss?"

In one lightning movement, she was free from my hold and had opened the door. "Behave, Mr. Jeansonne."

I'd never wanted to misbehave so much before.

The smile response from her feistiness was planted on my face the rest of the morning until I entered the dining room. I could hear the female chatter from the stairs.

It ended when I opened the door.

"What are you three up to?"

"It's our morning gossip," June answered with a warm grin.

"Morning gossip? Not about me, I hope."

My mother sighed and picked at a nonexistent speck on the tablecloth. "No, Delilah won't give us anything delicious to talk about."

Delilah choked on her coffee, more like milk with a drop of coffee. Red apple flush took over her cheeks and crept down her long neck. "I—I'm just going to be quiet."

The entire table laughed at her candor. My wife was a bright light in what had become a dreary routine. We'd all walked in a haze of aftermath for far too long.

"I have to talk to Rebel." I said, while sitting down at a breakfast I'd never intended on partaking in, but somehow found myself wanting.

"About what?"

"He's not cleaning the stalls properly." I answered my mother.

"Maybe that's because he's too busy chatting up our dear Delilah."

Every head popped up at attention at my mother's words. June excused herself at once, mumbling about something in the oven. I swallowed against the feeling of déjà vu in talking about Rebel. I'd hoped for his name to never grace our conversations again — at least in respect to my wife.

"You've been talking to Rebel." I couldn't help the accusatory tone I took with her. I was accusing her. It fit. Delilah blanched and squared off her shoulders.

"I went outside yesterday to get some fresh air and he approached me. The *conversation* was no more than four sentences."

I turned my glare onto my mother. I prayed this was a case of her overdramatizing events.

"He's also been watching you Delilah. I've seen it."

"Watching me what?"

"A few times I've seen him looking into your bedroom window."

Delilah clutched the opening of her shirt tighter together.

"What did he say to you?" I demanded in no soothing tone. I slammed my fist down with the words and everyone at the table shuddered, including me.

I thought Delilah would buck against my words and shout at me—maybe throw something. That was the spark I'd always loved in her.

Instead, I found her frozen across the table from me. She personified an animal in the pivot of a kill. Her chest moved in shallow burst with breaths of fear.

I was no better than her parents had been to her.

Disgusted with my behavior, I bolted from the table and went to the stalls, determined to push my disapproval onto the man who deserved my pointed words and anger.

"Rebel?"

He came out of the stalls from the other side. He hadn't been working, the smell of tobacco lingered in the air in a cloud around the back entrance.

"Yes?"

"These stalls need to be cleaned and you need to go pick up more feed. The appearance of this place is deplorable."

"I'm doing the best I can. What are you going to do, fire me?"

His sneer was laced with malcontent.

"It was my grandfather's contract. I'm sure we can find a way to break it."

"Come on, I don't do that bad of a job. Besides, your wife seems to enjoy my company — even more than Marie."

Anger pooled in my chest and flooded my veins. He was lying, that I was sure of. There was no sign of guilt in Delilah's eyes. The expression she pointed at me when I'd shouted at her for speaking to Rebel was that of a wife betrayed.

"You tarnished Marie. She could've been content here."

"Content? That's what every woman wants, contentment."

"Stay away from my wife." I ground out the words, pouring in as much contempt and threat as I was able to. "And clean out the damned stalls!"

Rebel didn't budge. He had defiant down pat.

Scrubbing a hand down my face, I made for the house. Before anything else, I had to figure out a way to get Delilah to forgive me for jumping down her throat. It wasn't her fault the sludge was watching her.

My fists clenched and relaxed with each step. I had to get control over my home. Before Delilah came, everything was calm and quiet. Marie haunted me only from a distance and only as the woman I'd almost married.

Rebel had done his job and kept his mouth shut before she came.

I'd reached out to help the helpless Delilah and threw my home into chaos.

I took three deep breaths before opening the door and finding out how many apologies would be necessary to redeem myself.

"Porter!" my mother screamed from the kitchen. I busted through the swinging door to find June and my mother, on the floor, hovering around Delilah.

"It just happened out of nowhere. She won't speak!"

They cleared, each focused on their own task. When they did, I got a look at what was happening while I was too busy with petty concerns.

My knees hit the floor first as my body crumpled at the sight. There were scratches, no gashes—three or four on each of Delilah's arms. She was unconcerned with them. She had her arms crossed, hugging her knees to her chest, much like she had when she'd been in the bathtub. Along with the blood on her arms, red rivulets ran down her mouth and chin from her nose.

"What happened?" I screamed at no one and everyone. June and my mother jumped at the booms, but Delilah never budged. Her eyes were glazed over and she stared at something behind me.

"She was helping us bring in dishes. And then it was like…"

"Something threw her against the wall." June and my mother had taken to finishing each other's sentences.

"Something can't just throw her against a wall!"

June tried to gently shove me out of the way to attend to Delilah, but I was having none of it. I scooped her up, blood and all, and carried her to our bedroom. We'd had the most wonderful night of my life and second by second, it was being ruined by forces beyond my control.

"I'm going to clean your face, love. Is that okay?"

She was oblivious to my words, maybe to my presence. Her eyes remained downcast while her chin quivered. I'd never seen a more pitiful sight.

There was no aggravation that could rival a foe that no one could see.

"Delilah, sweetheart, look at me. There's no one else here. I won't let anyone or anything touch you again."

Not knowing what to do and having few options, I got a cloth doused with frigid water and pressed it to her face, not for cleaning her up, but for breaking her out of this fugue state she was in.

She gasped out of nowhere, as though she'd been drowning and had finally surfaced. She clawed at me, grabbing the waist of my trousers, bringing me closer to her. I smoothed her hair and attempted to soothe her with my voice.

"I'm here. Nothing is going to harm you."

An hour passed before she would allow me to clean her up. The blood coming from her nose was nothing compared to the bubbling red liquid that continued to come from the slashes to her arms.

"We have to call a doctor, Delilah."

She shook her head, refusing the suggestion.

"Delilah, please," I begged. Maybe it was the sympathy in my heart. Maybe it was the heightened emotion of the entire afternoon. I'd never succumbed to begging before.

The light in my wife's eyes had dimmed, and that was enough to bring any man to his knees.

She squeezed my hands. The first of what would be many tears began to stream down her face. A sob was the first sound she'd made since the incident.

"Please tell me what happened. I can't help you if I don't know what did this to you."

After sucking in a deep breath, with her back straightened and her shoulders back, she told me.

"Marie."

Out of pure relent, I dropped my head into her lap and took advantage of the position that hid my face. My first instinct was disbelief. Marie had never hurt anyone in life, other than me, but that was more of a betrayal than purposefully inflicted damage.

"I don't understand, Delilah. I just don't."

"You don't believe me." Her voice had taken an aloof tone.

Grabbing onto her calves, I pulled myself up to look at her in the eyes. "I believe that you think you saw her."

She huffed out a rebuttal. "She doesn't look the same."

I breathed out a sigh of relief. This was all some mistake. Her observation did nothing to solve the issue, but at least we could chalk the whole thing up to her imagination.

"What do you mean?"

She stood, knocking me off balance. Her fists were clenched in anger behind her back.

"I mean she was older. She was thirteen, maybe fourteen. Her hair was longer. Her dress was not that of a child anymore. It was the dress of a teen. She had a white ribbon tied around her hair. She—she spoke to me."

Chapter Thirteen

Porter didn't believe me. Not only was it apparent in his face, but his eyes never told a lie. He wouldn't even look me in the eye.

The closeness, the surge of emotion, which had grown in my heart was one-sided.

I'd trust anything he said to me as complete truth.

Maybe that was my folly in life — I was too trusting.

"What did she say?"

I turned around briefly to find him now sitting on the bed, on the very edge with his face buried in both palms and his elbows resting on his knees. His thumbs massaged his temples. I was the headache he just couldn't get rid of.

Mentally, I congratulated myself on making it this far.

"She said, 'He's mine.'"

"Who was she talking about?"

I rolled my eyes at the always informed Porter asking me the stupidest question. There was no reason to dignify such an obtuse question.

"Me or Rebel?"

That question, however, was worth answering with a fist.

I didn't dare face him. My tears would only refute my answer. "You seem so determined to make me something I'm not—maybe someone I'm not. Ask yourself this, Porter Jeansonne. If I was loyal to people who neglected me most of my life, why would I become disloyal to the one person I've ever loved? Do not speak to me about Rebel ever again."

I steeled myself for his rejection.

"Delilah. I just don't…"

I didn't want to hear it. I couldn't' bear to hear the words. I'd traded one prison for another. At least at The Plots I'd be free to choose my poison. Here, I faced rejection—the house and its ghosts rejected me, and the knife that cut the deepest was that this man who'd saved me would never love me.

I'd become just like his mother. My happiness would be found in cake and ham instead of the people around me.

"Leave me alone, Porter—I beg you."

The words were constrained in my throat, but I forced them out anyway.

"I don't want to leave you."

I snorted. "Don't worry. I won't bleed anymore. And I promise not to see anymore ghosts — or at least tell you when I do. I've been alone all of my life. I can handle alone just fine."

He didn't move immediately. It took every ounce of strength I could gather not to collapse or just give in to the urges in my heart to cry.

Maybe I didn't want love after all.

"Please." His small plea annoyed me even more. Why would he want to stay?

I said nothing. My throat wouldn't allow it.

Minutes later, the click of the shutting door told me he'd gone. I slid along the wall to the floor, into a crumpled mess of tears and chest wracking cries into my thick skirt so no one would hear. I bit into the precious fabric and let the act take the brunt of my pain. I'd thought those days were long gone — the days where I hid my cries from listening ears and took solace in solitude.

I was wrong.

When all my tears were gone, I pulled myself up off the ground and tended to my wounds which were, in lieu of all the blood, superficial and resembled scratches more than cuts. I still hadn't figured out why my nose was bleeding.

It didn't matter. I could say that Marie shoved a crawfish claw up my nose and he wouldn't believe me. If I was smart, I would've really made the story extravagant.

If he wasn't going to believe me, the least I could do was have a laugh at it.

After a bath and a change of clothes, all filled with lingering whimpers, I decided to go in to the library to be alone. Porter was at his desk. He didn't even blink an eye at my presence, which was fine with me.

The ghost and I were the same—he could pretend neither of us existed.

A stack of books I didn't recognize sat on the couch. I fumbled through them, choosing one I'd never seen before with green leather binding. After retrieving my blanket from the arm of the couch, I tucked myself into a space between two bookcases. I didn't feel safe sitting anywhere my back was exposed.

It was a terrifying thought that your enemy was not only invisible to everyone around you, but could appear and attack without warning.

Resting my chin on my knees pulled against my chest, I didn't allow myself to get completely engrossed in the words though I desperately wanted to.

My stomach rumbled with the setting of the sun hours later. By the time the night came, I'd finished two of the books from the couch pile. I wondered why I hadn't seen them before. Maybe Porter had brought them home from the city.

Calling this house home brought unwarranted tears to my eyes again. The events of the night before and the day that followed barreled down on me, making me face it all.

For the first time in my life, I'd slept safe and sound in the inviting embrace of a man I thought would only ever tolerate my presence, yet seemed to genuinely care, only to have all of that unravel in a matter of a morning's time.

I wished he were there with me.

"Can I come in?" A knock on the door startled me.

Had I said the words aloud?

"It's your house."

He sighed, already aggravated with me. Even I was aggravated with the tone I'd taken.

"Why are you sitting there? Come sit by me. I can't stand this distance."

He sat down on the couch and opened his arm for me. I debated with myself. Being alone and frustrated was, in a disturbing way, my comfort.

It was futile. I was already under his spell.

"I'm sorry," he whispered into my ear after I sat next to him.

"I'm not a liar."

"I know. I think you're the only person in my life who always tells the truth. I want to hear everything."

We stayed there through the night. I told him everything about Marie, even speculating that the touches I'd felt here and there were her, trying to get my attention. And when those didn't work, she found other ways. I had my own hypothesis about the reasons for her appearing to me older and older, but I kept them to myself.

His face had gone completely white when I asked the same of him, to tell me everything about Marie.

"Are you sure you want to know?"

"I am. If we work together, maybe we can come to understand why she's attacking me."

Porter took my hands in his and shrugged before beginning. "Our marriage was arranged since I was a boy. Marie moved into the cabin near the back of the property after her parents died when she was eighteen, right before Christmas. We were to be married the following spring. I insisted we get married right away, but she was determined to have a spring wedding. She hated this house and said it was so depressing during the other seasons. It would be more like a funeral than a wedding. I showered her with gifts, trying to feed her insatiable wants. She loved the city, but after a few visits, I grew concerned about the hold it had on her. Marie began demanding things from me, money, clothes, and more every day. I was in a business meeting once and from the window of the room, saw her exiting a renowned voodoo shop. The woman in there had given her some concoction to keep her young looking. Of course, the first treatment was free. After that the price was too extravagant and we quarreled almost daily about her demands on me. I grew to detest her presence. Her voice was like the scream of an owl in my ears. I spent more and more time away from home—more and more time away from her."

The absence of his warmth was instant as he removed his arm from around my shoulders and wrung his hands together, gathering the courage to continue. It wasn't easy to hear the story of a woman who'd been promised to him as a boy. Porter deserved someone who appreciated every gesture of kindness he willingly gave. The only thing I would ever think about demanding from him was his heart.

His knee bobbed up and down.

It wasn't the first time I'd seen him pull that move.

"I came home on the morning of her nineteenth birthday, just a week before our wedding. We'd been fighting and I'd left angry. I searched all over the house and couldn't find her. My mother had gone to town with June. I finally..." His voice broke off. "In the pond. She was in the pond, face down. I tried—I tried to get in and save her, but it was much too late. Three days after the funeral I was rummaging through my desk for the keys to the cabin, when I found the note."

His Haunted Heart

Whatever the note contained, the thought of it brought him to tears. He stood and separated himself from me.

This man who held the reputation, even with his mother, of being a stoic and unfeeling kind, was broken. He had scars that ran so deep they couldn't be seen by the eye.

Some scars are too devastatingly beautiful for the world to see.

"Where's the note?"

My question caused him to stiffen in place. He was a statue and I was powerless not to look at the art of him. For a brief moment, I wondered what our marriage would look like if I wasn't who I was and he was free to be who he was without constraint.

Would he and I have met in the streets of the town?

Would he have even given me a second look?

"I will show you one day. I promise."

It wasn't what I wanted to hear, but it had been a long day and my head had been pounding for hours.

Doubling over, I wrapped my arms around the backs of my thighs and rested my forehead on my knees. I was cold again. The scratches on my arms had made themselves known little by little throughout the night. They screamed at me to heed their call.

"I'm such an imbecile. There's aspirin in the kitchen and you've got to be starving."

I looked down at the lines on my arms. I'd felt them, but hadn't looked at them since the incident, not wanting to see the face of Marie when I did. The lines were raised from my skin, angry.

I yawned so many times from the moment he dragged me from the library to the kitchen that tears flowed to the edge of my jaw, dropping off onto my blouse.

The rest of the early morning was a blur. I remembered eating and taking some pills from Porter, but that was the end of my memory.

A note was left between the two doors of my wardrobe. I saw it the next morning after I'd woken alone and cold in the bedroom that was ours in name only.

Porter had ridden to town to handle some business but would be back as soon as possible.

He still didn't believe me.

If he did, he would've recognized that the times when he was gone were the only times when the ghost of his un-beloved visited me.

My sleep was haunted by visions of the ghost of Marie and the note that seemed to be the core of Porter's disbelief about why she would haunt me.

I needed to find that note.

Bounding down the stairs, I noted the position of the sun in the sky, and realized it was much later than I'd thought. Porter may have been back any minute.

I took the key from the drawer where I'd found it before. As soon as I touched it, the gnarling of guilt gripped my insides and tried to sway me away from intruding on his privacy. The need to know more about what was my sworn immortal enemy was stronger than guilt. It was a matter of self-preservation. And while Porter was proficient in saving me from my parents and the cesspool of a life I'd been living in, this was one thing he was incapacitated in protecting me from.

I had to protect me.

And I had to make sure that the devil of a woman didn't turn her wrath on this man that I now loved.

I thought that was what marriage must be.

That is what I would make it.

Two people protecting each other.

My hands shook while I placed the key into the tiny lock and broke it free of the clasp. Inherently, I knew this was the place that held everything I needed to know about Marie and her insistence on tormenting my life after so many years of hovering harmless in Porter's.

It was as though I'd brought her to life.

Marrying me had been a catalyst that Porter hadn't bargained for.

I unfolded each piece of paper, one by one, careful not to bend or tear the delicate pages. Porter's birth certificate was there, along with our marriage certificate and my birth certificate. I hadn't even realized he had that one. All the things I didn't know about my own life troubled me and stirred worry in my heart.

I stared at the paper for more time than I was allotted by my husband's absence. My eyes were glued to the blank line next to Father.

"He gave it to me when you and your mother were making dinner. The night that I came to meet you."

Porter's voice made me jump and I dropped the small treasure chest-like box onto the floor, smashing it to pieces.

I squatted down and began to pick up the pieces, not knowing what his reaction would be to me snooping around. I didn't have to wait long.

"You're shaking."

His arms snaked around my waist and pulled me back from the mess. His breath was warm against my neck. It caused my shoulders to shake in shudder.

"My father's name is blank."

He pulled me tighter against his large frame and I sunk into his chest.

"You didn't know?"

"No."

"Look at me, Delilah."

The meaning of it all was crashing down on me, but I needed to hear the words. The small detail that would explain all the heartache and pain that was my life until Porter. It took a few moments before I was able to face him. Deep down, I knew what he was going to say.

I gathered my bravery and met his gray eyes, hoping that truth would set me free.

"Your father wasn't your biological father. That's what I was told. Your mother had an affair, early in their marriage."

The only reason I stayed sitting was Porter's hands on my arm and my back, holding me down.

"That's why they hated me."

"I don't know. I can't imagine a mother mistreating her child for that reason, especially when the reason points the finger right back to the one who had the affair. I can't tell you whether or not your sisters knew, though their blatant mistreating of you tells me they did."

I'd expected myself to cry over such a tragedy, but they never came.

"I didn't belong there. I belong to no one. I have no father. My family hates me. I couldn't even find a husband — at least one that wasn't willing to pay for me."

"Delilah Catherine Jeansonne, look at me. I'm going to say this once now and every moment until you believe it."

Must he demand eye contact for every word?

Again, I met his gaze, though inside, I was determined *not* to believe anything he had to say.

"I knew the first moment I saw you in that wretched home that you didn't belong there. You were like a withered magnolia among spiked weeds. You're right. You didn't belong with those people and you didn't belong with people who hated you. You belong with me. You will always belong with me."

He hadn't said he loved me, but it was the closest thing to love I'd ever felt. His words clenched my heart. It was more than I could take.

"One day I'll believe that."

"I won't stop telling you until you do."

Together we moved to pick up the pieces of the box. Porter gathered the papers and photos and stacked them in his hands. His face told me it wasn't something he was willing to face, but had to.

"I had to see the note. I have to know why. I'm sorry."

"It's okay. I've carried it by myself for way too long. Maybe you can help me with that."

He pulled out a picture and my gut instinct was jealousy. There were no pictures of me in his secret stashes. There wasn't a single picture of me in existence, even in my family home.

Marie was a beauty, more so in life than in death. She was older in the picture.

"How old was she here?"

"Eighteen. This was the Christmas before…"

"She's beautiful."

"She was. But only on the outside. Her soul wasn't beautiful—and before long, her soul was all I could see."

He took the photo from me and put it aside.

"This was us on her eighteenth birthday. This was when we officially began courting. Her parents insisted we take pictures together. They even had a fancy photographer come down here from Baton Rouge."

Porter looked like a different man in that picture. His shoulders were stronger. His eyes showed no signs of sleep deprivation or stress. Those gray eyes that stole my heart looked down at his then future bride with pride and devotion.

"You loved her."

"I loved the idea of her. I wanted a wife and a family, just like any other man."

"Do you still?"

"No." He paused. A smile grew on his face and I knew I'd been duped. "I already have a wife. Maybe one day she'll give me a family."

"If the ghost doesn't kill her first."

Silence took over the room. Something in the picture with Porter caught my eye. It was the necklace. I knew that necklace.

"Are there more pictures of Marie?"

He dragged his bottom lip through his teeth. "Yes, there's a box upstairs. Why?"

"I need to see them and then the letter."

He squeezed me once and placed a kiss at my temple. "I will get them. Take these and meet me by the fire. You've gone cold again. I'm failing on all fronts today."

He was failing on no fronts in my book.

I took the stack from him and we parted at the foot of the stairs. Not sure if Marie was found of the sitting room, I looked around for her presence just to make sure. I smiled to myself at the two chairs in front of the fire. One of those chairs, my chair, was the very spot that I first felt safe with Porter.

I supposed with us dragging out all of his past in the same place, it was time for him to feel safe sharing his secrets with me.

"Here's everything I could find."

He plopped an old box on the stool next to my chair. We thumbed through the pictures together. Since Porter was a child, most of his pictures either were with Marie or had her in the background scene. It was disturbing to say the least.

From adolescence to her teen years and beyond, Marie grew into a beautiful woman and I recognized her in some of the pictures where her appearance matched the apparition who'd tormented me.

All of those pictures, yet one thing never changed.

The locket around her neck.

The chains it was attached to changed. Once, in a picture on what Porter said was his sixteenth birthday, the locket hung from a bracelet. Nevertheless, it was always there.

"Did she always wear this?" I pointed to several pictures, highlighting the locket.

"Yes. I asked about it once. Her mother said it was given to her by a family friend when she was a baby. I always thought it was odd the way she never took it off. I asked her about it once. She threw a fit and accused me of trying to control her. I dropped the subject after that. It was just a necklace after all."

I didn't tell Porter that I'd seen that necklace or where I'd seen it before. I knew from the way he'd reacted this morning that Rebel's name threw him into a fit of anger, one that I never wanted to see again.

"Maybe you're right. Can I see the letter?"

That infamous letter was in my hands, but even more than looking for it, reading it in his presence felt wrong.

"You have it there." His hand shook as he pointed to the papers in my hand.

"But can I read it?"

"Of course."

I opened the letter, but before I could read anything past the word Porter, it was jerked from my hand.

"I'll read it to you."

"Are you sure?"

He nodded once and began. The words were clipped, almost child-like in nature. I could see the handwriting through the paper. Blots of ink dotted the I's. It looked more like a splattered painting than Marie's last letter.

I heard the words, but they failed to resonate with anything I knew about the man that read them. The hatred that spewed from the letter sounded more like she was addressing someone who'd attempted to murder her — or worse.

I interrupted him, not being able to handle any more. "You said you never treated her ill. You told me that despite your growing annoyance with her, you never behaved as such. You quarreled only because of her demanding more money. Isn't that true? Isn't that what you said to me?"

"Yes. I said that." Porter reached behind his head and scratched the back of his neck, like the whole thing confused him as much as it did me. "She must've been able to tell. I tried to hide it so well. My parents wanted nothing else for me than to marry her. I was trying to make them happy."

"And when she died?"

He shifted in his larger chair. "They seemed more relieved than I was."

"You should've spoken up, Porter. What would you have done, put up with being married to someone you didn't like just because your parents wanted you to?"

I'd sparked anger in him. His smoky eyes nearly came ablaze.

"I could say the same for you. If I hadn't come along, would you never have taken up for yourself?"

The weight of the impasse set me back in the chair, my hands wringing on the wooden arms.

He was right, of course.

"I'm sorry again. I promise, one day to go through an entire day without having to apologize."

He laughed, but I didn't. I didn't even care about myself anymore.

I didn't know if that was healthy or not.

The violins cradled in their stands and the piano tucked into the corner seemed to grow bigger as my mind ground through all the new information which brought on more questions than answers.

"Can we get out of this house? I feel like the walls are closing in on me."

He spoke the words that were brewing in my head.

"Please."

"We have a fishing pier at the edge of the property near the bridge. You may have seen it coming here."

I reddened thinking of riding behind Porter. I remembered thinking that he was the strongest man I'd ever known.

"I wasn't paying attention to anything around me—at least, not the landscape."

My husband reached out tentatively and then stroked my cheek with the back of his hand. "I love this color on you. If it were my choice, I'd have you blushing from morning until night."

I changed the subject. "You said something about fishing?"

I'd never been fishing, but I'd do anything to get out of these beautiful walls — every corner hid secrets and every turn of a knob or click of a window sent terrified goose bumps down my arms.

"Yes. I'll grab the fishing box and reels from the shed outside. Why don't you pack us up something to eat?"

These people and all their food.

Chapter Fourteen

I could barely breathe, the air was so thick with humidity. It hovered around us like a cloud full of impending rain. Delilah, on the other hand, was content as she'd been in my tree fort. Her legs swung back and forth in the same fashion. Her eyes mirrored the smile on her face.

I loved that about her; she found joy in peace.

It had been years, maybe a full decade since I'd told anyone that I'd loved them, including my own mother. The words were tacked to the end of my tongue, but I refused to let them be spoken. The sentiment was there, even in this short time. I wasn't one to believe in divine intervention, but Delilah coming into my life, despite the chaos, was a blessing I'd never asked for.

I was still looking at her when she slid two of her fingers down the bridge of her button nose.

"What are you thinking about?"

"Nothing, really."

"You touched your nose. Something is making you nervous."

She studied me for a moment and then turned away, pretending to be readjusting her fishing pole.

"You're still upset about your father? If you want me to ask your mother about your real father, I can do that. You don't have to see either of them ever again if you don't want to."

"You'd do that for me?"

"I'd do anything for you, including telling you how you're never going to catch anything if you keep moving your fishing pole like that."

Her anxious swinging legs were causing her fishing pole to bounce up and down in the water, making it impossible for any fish to ever get hooked.

"I've never fished before."

"Never?"

"Never."

"My father used to bring me here under the guise of fishing when he really had something important to say to me. I knew that as soon as I caught that first fish, he was going to go into whatever he wanted to say. Sometimes, I wished a fish would never bite."

Just as I finished my sentence, a tug at my line let me know that despite the anxious legs beside me, a fish had found my line.

After pulling it up, I let it go. I'd seen bigger fish in a sardine can.

"Don't laugh. You haven't gotten a single bite."

With a shrug, Delilah attempted to suppress her smile.

"It's your turn to tell me something profound. I caught the first fish."

"I know, or at least I think I know, why Marie is aging. I may not know why, but it correlates directly with something else."

She wasn't making any sense.

"What does it correlate to?"

"I'm not good at this."

I chuckled. "I know. You'll never catch anything."

In one fluid motion, she picked up the pole and tossed it, rod and bait, behind her.

"Not the fishing, Porter."

I had tried to prove to her that she could say anything, but my explosion at breakfast had torn that all apart.

In the distance, I heard a wagon and a horse that could only be mine. Benjamin always hastened his pace when he neared home. He seemed to be the only creature around that actually enjoyed this place.

"June and Eliza are back."

"So what? Tell me what you were thinking."

"We should go help them."

I grew exasperated with her unwillingness to let me in. I didn't deserve to be let in, but I wanted to, nevertheless.

"Fine, let's go help them. You're not off the hook, by the way." She bowed her head, hiding her smile from me, but I'd seen it. "And don't think I haven't noticed the lack of — affection, shall we say?"

"Behave, Sir. Your mother is right there."

We were speaking to each other through clenched jaws as we walked toward the approaching wagon. My mother had stayed in the main part of the house for far longer than I'd intended. But the closer and closer Delilah and I became the more I wanted privacy more than anything.

"I won't behave tonight. One night without you in my bed is one night too many."

By the time we reached the house, Delilah's face rivaled the redness of a cherry. I loved to make her blush. It was the one time I knew I was doing something right.

"Well, where have you two been off to?"

I cocked my eyebrow. "Fishing."

"Fishing? Not really the activity I was hoping for. I do want grandchildren someday, you know."

Delilah's eyes grew to the size of half dollars.

"Come on, Eliza, you've made the girl go whiter than she already was and that's saying a lot."

I kept Delilah close to me the rest of the day. Whether she liked it or not, I would keep her under my watch for the foreseeable future. After retiring to the sitting room after supper, I decided to play for her. I was desperate to win her heart—to keep her heart.

"I thought I'd play something for you."

"For me?"

"Yes, of course."

I moved to the piano in the corner of the room and cringed at the amount of dust on the fallboard. The ivory keys had spent too much time neglected, too much time unused. But as soon as my fingers hit the keys, the feeling of the music took over and the flood of emotion that emoted through the notes expressed everything I needed to say to my new wife, but couldn't. I supposed that was the point of music, an expression of words unspoken.

After a few songs, Delilah came to sit next to me, bringing a lone candle to sit atop the piano. That candle, plus the fire were the only lights in the room. The fire cast a light on her face that was unmatched in beauty.

The lower notes at the end of the song were dragged out on purpose, hoping that they carried meaning.

"That was beautiful. You should play more often."

"I will, if you like it."

"I love it."

"You want to play something?"

She ticked her eyes at the floor. "You know I can't play."

"Sit here." I scooted back and patted the space between my legs. It wasn't a big space, but even with my mother's prodding and pigging encouragement, she was tiny. Her breath hitched at my proposal.

"I don't know."

"My love, are you afraid of me?" I reached behind her head and threaded my hands in her hair at the base of her neck. The hair there held a softness that was incomparable.

"No. I'm not. I'm afraid of me."

My eyebrows showed her the question I couldn't express.

"I'm not good at this. This — intimacy."

Despite the coldness in the room, heated energy throbbed between us. My heart arrested with impatience. Her breaths, delicate yet bold, skittered across my skin, raising goose bumps.

"That's the whole point of marriage — to learn things together."

She ground her lips between her teeth. I would trade everything I owned to know what she was thinking at just that minute.

"It's just me, my love." I pushed every ounce of comfort I could into those words.

She scooted over and sat between my legs, her hands balled into fists, refusing to touch the keys.

Every time I exhaled, two ringlets at the base of her neck would waiver like Spanish moss hanging in a storm. Complete enamor trickled down my being as she turned her head to show me an innocent smile over her shoulder.

"I'm going to put my hands over yours and we'll play together."

I took my time, of course. Beginning at her shoulders, I skimmed my fingers along her arms leaving shivers in their wake. By the time my fingers overlapped hers, we were both holding our breaths, waiting for the complete connection.

We played the same song as I'd played before, but much slower. We fumbled through most of the piece until she withdrew her hands from mine and encouraged me to continue on my own.

With my chin rested on her shoulder, I played at her beckoning. Every once in a while, she would quiver in my hold while a playful grin encouraged me on.

Finally, as the moon rose higher in the sky and the candle's melted wax pooled around it, I finished my serenade to her.

"Those were the most beautiful sounds I've ever heard."

I took the opportunity to nuzzle her neck. I didn't stop there. My lips made a path along the base of her neck. I pulled down the curve of her shawl and continued my exploration along her shoulder blades and the space between.

She swayed with her back against my chest. I made my hands stay on her waist, not trusting them to move an inch in either direction.

"I would never hurt you, you know that, don't you?"

She nodded.

"Are you tired?"

No. She wasn't tired.

"What do you want?"

I was asking so much more than what she wanted to do for entertainment. I wanted to know what my wife wanted from me this night. What she would allow me to do.

"I just want you. I—I want you to love me."

She broke me with those words. I did love her. I loved how she'd melded into my life and I couldn't remember what I'd done with myself before she was here.

"Let's go to bed. You're shivering."

"It's not from the cold, husband."

We walked upstairs together, but trepidation filled me. We'd had no honeymoon concrete with expectations. We had just been strangers.

Except, she was part of me now.

"I can go to my room…"

She'd gathered her shawl back around herself on the walk to the bedroom. It was almost a force holding her together. Finally, she met my eyes.

"I don't want to sleep alone anymore. But it's your choice, Porter."

She turned and left, going through the bedroom door but leaving it open behind her. There was no choice.

Chapter Fifteen

After recovering from the shock of Porter in our bedroom for the first time, I ducked into the bathroom to change into a peach-colored nightgown, one of the ones he'd bought for me.

It was terrifying business, being married.

I walked into the bedroom and Porter stood at the window. His fingers were pressed to the glass. His face was clenched in a cathartic grimace of panic and disbelief.

"What is it?"

"It's—I can't believe it."

A pulse of anger worked through me thinking that Rebel was down there as June said, looking into our window.

"What is it?"

He didn't answer, but held his hand out to me while never breaking his gaze from the target of his attention.

I took his hand, clammy and tense, and sidled up next to him to share his vision.

Rebel stood on the center island of the pond, crouched with his hand stretched out toward the water. He spoke and if I had to guess, he was coaxing something or calling someone.

"It's the spot where I found Marie. What is he doing there?"

My breath hiked in response to what I saw next. Marie appeared in the water, head first, followed by the rest of her body, as though she were being birthed from the pond. Inch by inch, Rebel seduced her from the water with a flick of his fingers. A phantom hand, white and dry, despite the origin of her uprising, rose from the water and reached for him.

"They were in love in life. It must be true in death."

I watched in eager interest. I'd seen people in love.

He owned her, called her from the depths, and reeled her in from a place she didn't wish to leave. I could see the despair on her face. Even as she reached, her other hand stayed behind in the water.

He moved closer to the water and for a moment, I thought Porter was correct and that they would exchange some ghost to lover kiss of passion.

But Marie's hand moved beyond his outstretched one and to something closer to him — something around his neck.

She reached for the necklace.

It was there, around his neck, dangling out of his shirt, the gold shimmering by the light of the moon mixed with the haze that rested on the top of the water.

My mouth opened to tell Porter of my discovery, but he was already gone. I was sure his heart was broken by seeing them together again. She'd betrayed him in life and she was doing it again in death.

"Porter, I'm sorry."

"She's aged. You were right. All this time I doubted you. Most of me believed you, but this…"

"Even more today." I hadn't left the window or the scene below. Acid rose in my stomach and threatened to choke me. What had once appeared to be remembrance now revealed some kind of sick control.

Rebel took the necklace out and hung it in front of her with a pendulous motion. Marie bowed her head, her face and body now revealed a lady, maybe sixteen or seventeen at best. Her back and shoulders shook in sadness as he kept the necklace at arm's length, never letting her have it or even touch it.

He was torturing her.

She wasn't even allowed to rest in peace.

I moved the curtain open for a better view. I must've opened it too much because Rebel's eyes met mine across the pond and in an instant Marie's cries turned to anger as she seethed in my direction. Her attentions were now on me and in a movement that resembled gliding she swam across the pond and began toward the house.

But I was safe as long as Porter was with me.

I knew she wouldn't attack as long as he was near.

I approached the bed. Porter sat on the edge, bent over, head in his hands. He deferred to the stance whenever Marie was mentioned.

"I'm sorry. Her betrayal was unforgivable."

He shook his head in a disagreeing motion. "I have forgiven her. I just wish it would all end. I don't want you hurt and I'm sick of the past reliving itself, tormenting us both. I am worthless. I can't even protect my wife."

"We will figure this out, Porter. I'm sure of it. Let's go to bed. Everything will be brighter in the morning."

He looked up at me. I'd never seen a more pathetic look.

"What if we don't figure it out? Will you leave me? If you leave—I'll go with you. I'll sell everything here and we'll go wherever you want."

This man, who saved me from a broken and worthless existence, was now offering to uproot himself to make me happy.

"Let's go to bed. You're not thinking clearly."

He stood and his sheer height took my breath, yet he was the vulnerability in this duo.

"Which side do you sleep on?"

"The side next to you. I'm not particular, Porter. I'm simply grateful for a bed."

He chose the other side of the bed. I thought I might fall faint from the sight of him. I would never get tired of seeing Porter and knowing that he was my husband. We lay face to face, one of his arms under my head and the other lazy on my waist. His hands were always on my waist when underneath it all I wished for them to be somewhere else entirely.

"You said something to me earlier and I didn't answer you properly."

I traced a pattern on his chest with my finger. I'd said lots of things to him earlier.

"What did I say?"

"You said you loved me."

I raised up on my elbow and looked down on him, now on his back. My hair gave me some protection until he pushed it behind my back.

"I said that."

"Did you mean it?"

"I don't say things I don't mean, Porter."

He paused. The atmosphere had changed around us. The curtains were drawn around the bed and even in the pitch black, I knew he could sense the smile in my words.

"Say it again." His demand came with a tightening of his arms around me.

I waited a breath—then two. This felt different, like saying those words would surely tangle me up further in his grasp.

"I love you, Porter. I think I have since the moment you walked into my home."

A bloated silence filled the space after my confession. A little part of me died along with it. I'd dared to hope for his heart-filled response, but got nothing.

"I love you, Delilah. I have since you made me hide against the tree so you could climb the ladder."

I laughed, louder and more boastful than I thought possible. "I still owe you for that. You never called in your favor."

"I want to call it in now. Would that make me horrible?"

Before I could answer, his lips were on mine and I was under him, the weight of his body feeling like heaven.

No, making me his didn't make him horrible at all.

The next time I saw Porter was at breakfast. He'd given me the morning to myself, which I appreciated.

His
Haunted
Heart

All night, despite how tired I was, I thought about Marie and Rebel and that necklace, the one that seemed to call her from the grave. (elaborate. She feels complete and loved)

Chapter Sixteen

I reached over her sleeping body and opened the curtains. Though it was dark in our cocoon, I'd stayed lying silent next to her just listening to her breathe in and out. I'd had to contain my chuckle several times as she made noises when she turned left or right. I half-expected her to wake up in a panic. It was only the second time we'd slept together and the first time for everything else.

The sun came through the curtains and gave me a whole new perspective on my wife, now truly my wife.

"Delilah, my love, it's morning."

I laughed as she pulled her hair over her face, shielding her eyes from the morning.

"I have some things to tend to. I thought maybe you'd like some privacy this morning."

She froze in place. Maybe the events of the night before were finally catching up to her waking consciousness.

I moved some of the hair from her face and saw that I was right. Her blush was furious and I'd put it there.

"Come on, you didn't forget that easily, did you? If not, I need to remedy that."

"I remember it all."

She murmured the sentiment, but I'd heard it.

"Good. I'll get dressed and you can take your time coming down. Unless you'd rather me bring you something to eat up here?"

"No!" was her ardent reply, which made me laugh even harder.

"Would you send me off like this? Without even a morning kiss?"

Then my timid yet courageous wife surprised me more than I ever knew possible. She sprang from the covers, without a fleeting attempt to cover her bare skin and threw her arms around my neck. For what seemed like the most glorious morning hours, she kissed my face from forehead to chin and back again.

"Will that last you awhile?"

One side of her mouth tipped up in a devilish smile that had me rethinking the entire concept of breakfast.

"I could always stay here and help you get dressed for the day."

Her eyes turned downward. "Maybe another time. Just give me this first morning alone."

I sighed. "If you insist."

"Thank you."

She lay back down on the bed while I got out and got dressed. I was well aware that her eyes never left my form as I did.

"Getting your eyeful?"

"You would leave me without a peek?"

"I guess not."

Before I could turn around, I heard the door to the bathroom shut and the water turn on. I took the liberty of bringing down the sheets myself, wanting anyone else tasked with the chore. June wouldn't dare say a word. It was my mother who I'd worried about.

Downstairs, I decided to pay Rebel a visit and make myself clear if I hadn't the day before. When I entered the stalls, I found the place immaculate with sacks of food stored and fresh water for all of my horses.

He'd gotten my point, and that was the main issue.

I took my time going back to the house, giving my wife the time she needed to take care of herself.

Somehow everything had solidified the night before without words.

I had to figure out how to protect her and get rid of the woman who had never owned my heart. And the next time I was in town, I had to get rid of Rebel. My lawyers would know how to take care of expelling the contract between our families. If nothing else, I would offer him a decent sum of money. If I'd learned nothing else from marrying Delilah, it was that money could buy so many people here in The Rogue, where the green in people's eyes wasn't just from the reflection of the lily pads.

I found myself near the back of the property and I could see Delilah in the window of our bedroom, brushing her hair. She turned to the right and inspected her face.

I couldn't even remember what the scar looked like anymore.

I didn't see anything but her eyes, the roundness of her nose, the long length of her neck and how much she loved my mouth there.

My legs made the decision for me. I was drawn to her like a mosquito to blood.

There was no point in resisting.

I met her at the foot of the stairs.

"Hungry?"

"Yes."

I folded her hand in my arm. There was no mention of anything scandalous at the dinner table and if my mother had a notion as to the night before, she didn't give anything away.

"I was talking to June this morning about finally moving to the mother-in-law house."

I nodded in agreement. That was the original deal.

Delilah spoke up. "Do you have to?"

"Well, I don't have to, but it's the usual protocol. I stayed for a bit to make sure you were eating and taken care of. I knew Porter would be gone soon after your wedding. But I think it's time to go."

There was a sadness I hadn't taken the time to consider in my mother's eyes.

"If it's okay, I'd like you to stay here."

Even Delilah looked shocked to hear her claim.

"Are you sure? Porter?"

I didn't say anything right away, so Delilah defended her claim. "Porter, when you are out of town, I'll be here alone. I've been alone all my life."

"I'm fine with it if it makes you happy, love."

"There." She patted my mother's hand. "That settles it."

June and my mother sat silent. June's fork was still halfway to her mouth.

Delilah went back to eating her eggs as if the world hadn't just tilted a little in her favor. We listened to June's latest stories and I told the women at the table some of my old stories. It was a delight to see Delilah ask questions and gasp at the parts that were old news to the others.

"Can we take a walk? I feel like I need some air."

"Of course. Let's go out the back."

As soon as we were out of sight, I pressed her against the nearest tree and kissed her until both of us were breathless.

"I thought you said you'd last the morning?"

"I lied. I don't think I'll ever get enough of you."

She dragged me away and until the late afternoon we walked around the property. She smiled all the way, asking questions and making observations.

"May I ask you something?"

She stopped but looked the other way.

"You can ask me anything, Delilah. I thought we'd moved past this."

"Can I see my sisters? Can we invite them here? I have to know."

"If that's what you want, but I have some conditions."

She seemed surprised. It was unbelievable to me that after everything we'd come to know about her family that she would still have anything to do with them.

"I have to be present and you are not to be alone with them at any time. I won't budge on that issue."

"I wouldn't expect anything less from you."

I heaved out a weighted breath. I hadn't realized it, but her approval of me as a husband was something I strived for.

"Thank you. We can send a formal invite or we can go to your old home."

"No. I don't want to go there. Everything changed last night, Porter. I knew that I loved you, but…"

I stopped her at a bench by one of the large cypress trees and pulled her down beside me. "But what? What else changed? Did I do something?"

She smiled. Blood rushed to her cheeks and neck.

"What I mean is, there is now the possibility of a child. My thinking has changed. This morning, do you know why I protested your mother leaving?"

"Because you didn't want to be alone."

"Because I didn't want to be alone, and if one day there is a baby, I'll need help. I can tell you everything there is to know about how to not be a mother, Porter. In terms of being a good mother, I haven't the faintest idea."

Not being able to stand the small distance, I closed it and dragged her over to my lap. She was my undoing, heart and soul. I was right, she had tomorrow in her eyes all along. "We will do this together, Delilah, if there is to be a child. If there isn't, I will just spend the rest of my days loving you and that will be enough."

"Together?"

Most men in The Rogue and even in the cities took little effort in raising their children, but my father was involved in my care from the beginning. I intended to do the same by Delilah. She hadn't brought the child, or future child, into the world on her own. I'd be damned if I left her to raise it by herself so I could pursue other things.

Even if I never worked another day, we were set for life and even our children would be set for decades.

"Yes, together."

"I'm getting ahead of myself. I just woke this morning with the aftereffects bearing down on me."

Before I could assure her any further, I heard June calling me from the house.

"Come with me."

She fidgeted and pulled her infamous nose move. "I'll just stay here a little longer. You'd better go see what's the matter."

I ran to the house and listened for a half an hour about how the bacon June had gotten from the butcher wasn't up to par. Apparently, there was some long-standing quarrel between the butcher and her. By the time she finished bludgeoning my ears with her rant, I'd gotten a headache.

"And I ran into that God awful father of hers too. He tried to get me to buy a roast for him, saying he'd left his money at home."

I shook my head, bringing myself back into focus.

"He spoke to you? How did he even know who you were?"

She shrugged. "I don't know."

"What did you tell him? You didn't give him any money, did you? I don't want him harassing you."

She pounded the cleaver she was using into the butcher board and pointed her finger at me like she'd done when I was just a boy. "Let me tell you, Porter Jeansonne, I don't let anyone run over this family and I'll be damned if I ever give a thing to that man or his family that treated that sweet girl like dirt. I'll make a roast out of him before he gets a dime."

A proud smile grew on my face. My wife was loved and respected in my home. Even if I did have to go to work, I knew that Delilah would be safe.

Now, if I could only keep Marie away from her.

"Thank you, June. You know you're like a second mother to me."

"That counts with you too, you know. I see you actin' a mess around Delilah like you did the other morning and I'll...well...you don't mess with the woman who makes the soup. You get my drift?"

I tucked my smile back and nodded. "Yes ma'am."

"Speaking of, where is the girl?"

"Outside."

"She's spent enough time alone. And you're in my way." June shoved me out of the kitchen. I decided to give Delilah a few more minutes alone when a knock resounded at the front door. I rolled my eyes at the sight. Delilah's older sister, I didn't recall her name, stood outside, assessing the paint job on my house, using her fingernails to chip at the boards beside the door.

We were so foolish, thinking of inviting people who obviously had no concept of basic manners.

I would consider this their last visit, invited or not.

I thumped my head on the door just for good measure before opening it.

"Hello…"

"Adele," she finished for me. "It's no wonder you don't remember our names. The wedding was handled in such a rush. I missed seeing my sister the next day."

My mind conjured a name for this family member that my manners wouldn't allow me to utter.

"Once I met her, I couldn't stand to be away from her one more second. I'm sorry I swept her away from the family so quickly. Please, come in."

She propped her tattered umbrella by the door and didn't bother to wipe her feet. June tried in vain to scurry from sight, but Adele had already made herself at home. "You there. I'd love a good cup of tea or coffee. I'm sure you have some made. I've come through all this weather to see my dear sister."

The sun peeked out from the clouds to call her on her blasphemy.

"Delilah is in the garden. Let me go get her. You wouldn't want to exert yourself any further."

"Yes, please. I'll just take a seat by the fire."

A hand over my mouth covered my snicker. I tramped outside to find Delilah and give her enough time to prepare her questions and concerns to her sister. She wasn't by the bench where I'd left her, and like the first night that I couldn't find her, a swirl of panic began to tornado in my gut. Fast-paced walking turned into running and mild-mannered yelling her name grew into frantic screaming of her name. My mind went to the pond and I scanned the surface, sure I'd find her and already harboring the guilt of two lives.

"Porter, I'm here."

I barely restrained myself from running to her. She was on the back porch and by the shock on her face I assumed she'd heard me calling out for her.

And it was then that another cry caught my ears.

I turned to see Marie, rising from the pond's blurry surface, mouthing words unheard, with her eyes fixed on Delilah.

"Go inside, Delilah."

Marie's head turned toward me and anger brewed in her yesterday stare.

"Go inside." I ground out through a clenched jaw.

"Come with me. I won't go in unless you come with me. She doesn't hurt me when we are together."

Her words snapped me to attention. It was as if her voice overrode any notions of me trying to approach Marie.

I took the steps in one motion and joined her, my purpose renewed.

"You've seen your sister."

She sidled up next to me and beckoned me downward with her fingers. The heat pulsed between us even in these circumstances. It was undeniable and her instant blush told me it was palpable to her as well.

She put her mouth to my ear and giggled. "I heard her nasal voice from outside. I never realized it was that loud. I'm surprised she didn't try to flirt with you. I would've loved to see your face."

Cheeky—that was the word for her—cheeky.

"Would you? I can guarantee you it wouldn't even be close to the face I made when you…" The rest of my sentence made her gasp.

A job well done.

"You're okay with seeing her?" We moved at a snail's pace toward the sitting room.

"You won't let her slash me with a knife again, will you?"

I halted, struck down by her bold statement. Humans, I had no trouble protecting her against.

I had to find a way to protect her from *everything* that threatened her.

"I'm just kidding, Porter. It's best you sit closest to her. I have a feeling her words will make me want to give her a bit of a shove into the fire."

"Were you like this before?"

One of her eyebrows cocked. "Like what?"

"Funny and…" The other secret characteristic, I whispered into her ear, reveling in the gasp it caused.

I bit the inside of my cheek as my blushing wife collected herself. Without permission, I took her arm and led her into the sitting room where we both stopped cold, shocked at what we saw next — the audacity.

Adele, I wanted to be childish and call her ASmell or something equally immature — sat in Delilah's chair with her bare feet propped up on my chair. Crumbs of all kinds left a trail down the front of her dress. Her jacket was unbuttoned from her gluttonous affair and a puddle of coffee spread out on the skirt.

Yet Delilah was the shunned member of the family.

"She must've been tired."

"And hungry."

"And cold."

"Should we wake her?"

"I feel like she's the giant that shouldn't be woken, but then again, I want her here as little time as possible. Once mother finds out she's eating her best shortbread cookies, she might carry your sister out over her shoulder like a sack of potatoes."

The word potatoes must've stirred something in Adele, because she woke up with a snort.

"Oh, Delilah, finally you're here, dearest sister."

Dearest sister was new to Delilah, I could just tell by squint of her eyes.

There were also the remnants of their sisterly love down the side of her face.

I expected one of Delilah's infamous quips, but instead, she'd clammed up beside me until I squeezed her hand and reminded her of where she was and who she'd become—I hoped.

"Adele, what brings you here?"

"Well…" she sat up, offended, by the swift movement of her hand up to her neck. "I didn't realize I had to announce a visit to my own sister and her new husband."

I stepped in, already tired of her antics. "Adele, as you realize, we are still in the honeymoon phase of our marriage. From now on, I think it appropriate if you give us at least a day's notice."

Every cheek in the room reddened, including June who had just stepped in when I began my oration.

"I will make note to do that from now on. Porter, dear, would you mind giving Delilah and I some privacy? I'd like to speak to my sister of womanly things."

"I'm sorry. I'm not comfortable leaving Delilah on her own yet."

As if I'm not irritated enough, a fluttering of fluid shadowed movement catches my eye. It's crawling from corner to corner and I can't help but think that this devil woman in front of my fire brought the damned thing in with her.

No one else in the room was fazed by the shadow, so I continued.

"Let's sit down and hear your sister out."

The alternative was paying attention to that dreadful chain around my chest.

I needed time away from all of this foolishness to end a ghost—which was foolishness in itself.

"I have just been feeling wretched lately, Delilah."

Under her breath, June muttered, "*Not enough to nip her appetite.*"

"Oh?"

"Yes, there's something I need to tell you about, well, about your husband."

Chapter Seventeen

I'm neither in the mood or the disposition to hear any of Adele's crap today. Pretending to loosen my shoulders, I look at Porter to assess his attitude about the whole thing. Not days earlier, he had insisted these people weren't allowed in our home.

Maybe he'd let Adele in based solely on her beauty.

"You need me to rub your shoulders?"

Porter was in a world all his own. He hadn't given Adele's dramatic bursting faze him in the least.

"Maybe later. Let's hear what Adele has to say."

My sister closed her eyes and while she primped and prepped herself for the big reveal, the shadow passed in front of the fireplace and caused the flames to dance in warning. The muscles in my stomach pulled taut as I did my best not to show alarm.

The Rogue would be rich in gossip for months.

Porter's hand slipped under mine and gripped it tighter. He'd seen the shadow too and for once I was relieved.

"I had wished to use a little more discretion in telling you this, but it seems I cannot. It is rumored that Porter has been visiting some very interesting places while he is in the city. Places I'm sure a married woman wouldn't want her husband visiting."

I cleared my throat. "Town gossip or did you see him with your own eyes?"

"Actually, it was Father who heard it from the Constable. They were very concerned over your reputation and that of your husband, of course."

Eliza entered the room sometime after Adele began and as she listened on, her cheeks began to redden and puff out.

She would need more cake soon, I could feel it.

"How dare you? My son has never been anything but upstanding and honest with his wife. I'm sure of it. Porter, I thought we agreed that these *people* weren't allowed in our home any longer."

"These people?" Adele was, maybe for the first time in her life, offended.

"Yes, these people. Delilah is our family now and we don't put up with persons who wish her harm, in the present or the past."

"Diverting the subject away from your dear son, I see."

My sister picked dirt out of her finger nails with the edge of the teaspoon. I'd never realized, despite their outer attractiveness, how foul Adele was. Yes, I knew she was hateful and unkind, but really she was a beast of a girl.

From my perspective I could see how her nose was upturned a little, resembling a pig. Her arms were gangly and much too long for her frame.

"Adele, if there's nothing else. I think it's time for you to leave. You've upset my household once again and I won't stand for it."

"But I have more to say!" she shouted.

"Then say it and be done."

"There's also a rumor that his fiancé and the stable boy had hired a crawfisherman to kill Porter after the two schemers were married for a measly ten dollars. If he hadn't driven the poor girl to kill herself, he would've done it. That swamp smelling killer is telling everyone who will lend an ear that our dear Delilah will come to the same fate."

I rolled my eyes as she pretended to be grief stricken by the very idea. Looking down, I realized Porter had released my hand. As I trailed my eyes up to his face, I was shocked to see his jaw grinding back and forth and his hands atop his thighs in fists.

It was one thing for Adele to come in and upset me, but to upset these other people was uncalled for.

This was my family now and while I'd had no backbone in my younger days—that had all changed in the span of a few short weeks.

"Get out!" I rose and pointed toward the door.

"Excuse me?" Adele used to say that all of the time.

"No. I won't. Get out of my house."

She stood and swiped at invisible crumbs on her shoulder when she should've been swiping at the clearly visible ones on her skirt. "This isn't your house. Don't be a fool, Delilah."

"This is her home. Her name is on the deed and her name is attached to all of my money. Anything I owned, own, or will own is hers. If she says get out, I suggest you comply before I get involved."

His voice shook. He was still rattled from whatever Adele referred to before.

"I won't be visiting anymore if this is how you're going to treat me."

"You weren't welcome to visit in the first place, Adele."

With my hand on her elbow, I pulled, rather than escorted her to the door where Eliza and June were already standing at the ready with it wide open. The only thing wider were their grins.

"I—wait—I don't have money for the man who brought me here."

Porter pulled out some bills and held them in the air for her. With a snide mumbling, she snatched them from his hand and never looked back. We all stood there and watched as she got smaller and smaller in our minds and in our vision.

We proceeded through the rest of the day in silence. Porter hadn't said a word about Adele's telling and I hadn't asked. He would tell me in good time and I would believe him.

I had no choice.

My heart had no choice in the matter.

The back porch called to me and so did the Louisiana night air. I sat in one of the rockers and let the lull of the back and forth motion calm me. I didn't wonder about the first part of Adele's confession. Porter didn't strike me as the type to visit prostitutes if that was even what she alluded to.

Maybe there was something even more sinister in the city.

I'd never know. The city had always been like a dungeon to me—some may be curious, but I was not.

I'd seen a little of hell.

I didn't want to go back.

As I looked beyond the once-white railings on the porch and out to the pond, I noticed movement along the other side of the porch. Someone was in the grass.

"Who is there?" I called, chastising myself for not sounding bolder.

"Rebel."

Of course it was Rebel.

"What are you doing skulking around? Shouldn't you be gone for the day?"

He took a few minutes coming to the stairs of the porch, looking down the entire time. He searched for something.

"I've misplaced something — important to me."

"What is it? I'm sure it's here somewhere. It's getting dark, you'd better find it before then."

The chagrin on his face unsettled me.

"I have to find it before night falls. I don't know what will happen if I don't."

He talked to himself more than me. His face was red and splotchy from worry, I guessed.

"Rebel, I'm sure we can find it, but I can't if I don't know what I'm looking for."

"It's none of your concern. I had it in the stable."

Without alerting him, I pressed Marie's necklace against my chest, just to make sure I still had it. As if I'd conjured her with the movement, her form emerged from the line of fog along the water, but this time she was an entirely different creature.

Her skin sagged off of her face in clumps of wrinkles. Her hair, once shiny and bright now slithered like snakes from her head, wet and clumped into chunks that threatened to fall out with the slightest tug. Her dress and that ribbon in her hair remained the same.

"I'll find it Marie," he whispered. His voice had taken on a tone that matched Marie's appearance.

"What will you find?" Porter's tone startled me, causing me to jump in the chair.

"Nothing. I lost something that belonged to me."

"Better than something that belonged to me, I guess. Then again, you're good at losing things that belong to me as well."

"Shut up, Porter!" Rebel hissed.

"Go home, Rebel. The night is already coming in. You won't find anything tonight. I'm sure the squirrels won't steal whatever you've lost."

"Fine. I'll be back at the break of dawn."

"That will be a first."

Rebel shot Porter a glare that was meant to be deadly but stalked off anyway, swearing until we could no longer hear him.

"I want you to stay away from him — please." The 'please' came after several seconds of pause.

"Porter, I came out here to get some air and he was in the bushes looking for God only knows what. He looked distraught and then…" My voice trailed off as I noticed Marie was no longer in her place or anywhere at all for that matter. "Marie was there."

"Do you want to come inside?" He looked around, now concerned about my ghost sighting.

"No. I'm enjoying the cool air. Why don't you come sit with me? You look like you've got a hundred ghosts in that head of yours."

He said nothing but sat in the chair next to me. It was a his and hers set, the woman's rocked and the man's did not.

Women needed rocking chairs for babies and for their nerves.

"I don't care what she said about you, if that's what you're so sullen about."

"Sullen? Is that what you think I am?"

"Yes. You're not speaking to me. You've been avoiding eye contact."

He leaned forward and raked his fingers through his black hair. There was nothing more I wanted to see at that moment than those gray eyes, but he refused. "I'm worried, Delilah. Didn't you hear what your sister said? It's all beginning to make sense now—well, not really, but it's got me thinking."

"You're not making any sense."

"Don't you see? From the moment Marie got here, she was preoccupied with Rebel—where he was—what he was doing. She claimed it was all friendship. But I knew better. She was adopted, did I tell you that? She was—at the age of five. Even her parents were weary of her behavior. Delilah, what if it's true? What if she'd planned it all along, marrying me and then killing me off just to take my money, my property, and she'd get Rebel as a parting gift."

"Honestly, I don't know. But if that was the plan and it was working, why did she kill herself?"

I kept my own notions to myself about Marie and that note.

"Something must've changed her mind. Maybe she felt guilty and decided that was the only way out."

"Are you interested in my opinion on the subject?"

"Of course, Delilah."

"Well, you said Marie was raised here and sent to the best of schools. I've seen several of her letters and yet the one she wrote to you looks as if it were written by a completely different person—not even a woman."

From his troubled post, he turned to face me. Lines of distress marred his otherwise handsome face.

"Are you saying she didn't write it?"

Everything he'd believed for who knows how long was being untangled and unraveled in one question. I didn't even have to answer it for him to see the truth in my quiet.

"It never occurred to me. I took it at face value."

"Porter, you and I know better than anyone to accept things at face value. Often they are the opposite of truth."

The night descended on us. The crickets signaled our bedtime, but it came and went as he rolled the events of the day through his head over and over again. I understood his pain.

"Porter, let's get to bed. You're accomplishing nothing by sitting out here punishing yourself. We'll figure all of this out."

"Will we?"

"It's the least I can do. I've brought so much strife on your house."

For once, I was the one comforting him through the scars.

I took his silence as agreement.

Chapter Eighteen

Rebel shows up at the most peculiar moments. If he was smart enough to have a gift, that would be it.

There's always been something about him that crawled down my spine. It was the way he looked at people when they weren't paying attention. It was the way he never kept regular hours—always here in the mornings or at night when the last thing you wanted to see was his face.

He skulked around the property. He was more a ghost than Marie herself.

What circumstances forced my grandfather into signing a contract that cemented us into giving his family permanent employment was beyond me. They'd all given pathetic efforts at their work.

Then again, it would cost me three times as much in attorney fees as it did his annual salary to get out of the contract.

I didn't like the way his eyes grew darker when he looked at Delilah.

I hated the way everything I knew crumbled to pieces, the more I learned about Marie and Rebel.

When I'd seen Delilah in that shamble of a house, frail and weak, I wanted to save her more than anything I'd ever desired in my life.

Yet, here she was letting me lean on her like a crutch.

On the other side of the closet, that was as large as the smaller bedrooms, I watched her undress. Much had changed between us. She no longer clung to me—she stood more confident—her posture revealed a self-assured woman instead of the oppressed creature I'd found that night.

The night that changed my life.

I watched as she took a necklace off and shove it into the top drawer of her dresser.

"I never noticed you wearing a necklace." I mentioned, turning around to toss my shirt over the top of a chair.

"I—I found it."

"It must be my mother's. She left some things here for you. I'm glad you like it."

I heard the swish of the tie on her robe and her feet pad across the Cypress floor, onto the rug, and back to wood again. Before she reached me, I felt the hairs on the back of my neck rise. My chest tightened as she came near, every time.

"You're okay?" Her question was coupled by long and lithe arms encircling my waist. She pressed her cool face between my shoulder blades. As she spoke, her breath skittered along my skin.

It broke me.

"I just wanted to save you—bring you to my home and take care of you—even if you never loved me or even liked me. It's all gone to hell now."

"She hasn't been around much since—since the last time. Maybe something happened to make her stop. The way I see it, the good far outweighs the bad."

I brushed off her sideways compliment and the kiss on my shoulder that went with it.

"If the note wasn't her writing—do you think Marie was murdered?"

"What other reason would there be for someone else writing a suicide note?"

Her tone grew more and more disenchanted as the days drew on. Before long, the angel that had by accident come into my life would grow to despise this life if I couldn't put an end to the constant upheaval around us.

My name, once sapid on her tongue would sour and grow to be a bitter word in her mouth.

Like Marie's name had become to me.

"I don't know. I don't want to speak on the matter anymore."

She giggled, letting go of my waist and rounding my body to stand face to face with her husband.

"I would be happy to let it go if you would stop bringing it up, husband."

A bit of laughter huffed from my nostrils at the word. It still had a breath of honey coming from her. Not too late to salvage my wife's love.

As we strode into the bedroom, I noticed her wardrobe and the drawers to her vanity were open. After asking her to stay behind me, I investigated. Nothing was misplaced and the clothing and items inside the open drawers and cabinets were untouched.

"Maybe your mother has been in here looking for something." In desperation, Delilah attempted to rationalize the out of turn incident.

"She was looking for something but moved nothing?"

Now I was the one who sounded haunted.

"Let's go to bed. I can't think about this anymore."

She crawled into bed without a second look in my direction.

It was then I realized how the tables had turned. Once, I sought her in some misplaced sense of heroism or redemption only to find that now she was the one who held my entire being in the palm of her hand and my soul was wrapped around hers.

The creature that once needed saving had saved me from a purgatory I'd damned myself to.

Before my head hit the pillow, I felt the wracking sobs coming from the docile creature beside me.

Oddly enough, I felt honored that she would show me such emotion. For years, I knew, or I assumed, her emotions or any outward show of emotions were kept to herself. Her crying was saved for dark corners or solemn moments of peace.

"You don't have to cry by yourself anymore, love."

My voice took her by surprise. She froze in place and tried in vain to squash her rapid breathing.

"Delilah, if nothing else, allow me to hold you while you cry. I'll be damned if I can change the things happening around us, but I can hold you and keep you. Or I can leave if you wish me to."

Her body flipped and she faced me again. I swore that every time I looked at her, another feature became apparent. At that moment, I could see a triangle of freckles by her collar bone.

I hadn't seen those before.

I was a fool.

"I will never wish for you to leave, Porter. As much as I never wanted to get married, or never thought I had the chance of getting married—there's nowhere else I'd rather be."

"Do you mean that?"

"I do."

Her confirmation rang with the truth that her first 'I do' should've. With the truth of concrete emotion behind it.

I pushed one stray strand of hair behind her ear. She pulled it back down immediately, still trying to cover up a part of her that I'd grown to love just as much as the rest of her.

"Does it ever pain you?"

"Every once in a while. It stings—here." She pointed to the top where the deepest cut must've occurred, at the very start of the jagged line.

"Maybe there is still something a doctor could do."

"It reminds me. It used to remind me of horrible things and nasty people. But now it reminds me that those days are long gone."

I couldn't help the chuckle that burst from my mouth. This woman was intelligent and wise beyond her years. Anyone who looked beyond her decrepit home and her dreadful family would've seen the angel that stayed tucked into the corners of her own hell.

"You are beautiful." I whispered down to her. I'd shifted to rise above her, partly covering her with my body.

She blushed but did not disagree. Her lips, full and ripe begged for mine. Her tongue ran a haughty path along the bottom lip as eyes the color of the sky itself gazed at me in a way that no woman ever had.

"Porter?"

I answered her with a groan of sorts.

"Close the curtains."

Chapter Nineteen

After a fitful night of sleep for the both of us, we barely spoke until both of us had ingested enough coffee for a week.

"I was thinking of going to the city today," Porter said. The word city made me frightened as a girl. Now as a married woman, it made my stomach turn. "I thought maybe you'd like to come with me."

I looked at both June and Eliza whose smiles seemed to encourage the venture.

"For how long?"

"A couple of days. Three at the most."

I was sure that a visit to the city would seem like a vacation to most, but for someone as obscure as myself, it was yet another place to hide my scar and duck from unwelcome stares.

"No harm will come to you, as my wife."

"Oh yes, Porter is very important in the city. He is well-respected and listened to. You'll see."

Eliza spoke as if the decision had already been made.

"All the reason for him to go alone," I muttered under my breath.

Porter had impeccable hearing.

"I changed my mind. I'm insisting you come with me."

Just weeks ago, I would've folded under that subtle command. Firmly intending to rebel against his insistence, my arms crossed over my chest—until I looked into those gray eyes.

Any mutiny I thought I'd built up was squashed.

"When do we leave?"

In vain, he attempted to squander a smile. "As soon as you can get packed."

Not wanting to seem too enthusiastic, I waited a few minutes until Porter went to his office to burst up the stairs and look for a bag. I didn't even know what to pack.

Eliza came in wordlessly and plopped a huge leather suitcase on the bed. I stood in the middle of the bedroom, helplessly as she packed for me.

"These boots are unworn. Walking on the concrete of the city is different from walking on the land. You'll want to wear your worn boots. They will be more comfortable."

She went on and on as she neatly packed everything I would need for a week or more. She didn't touch Porter's things and I assumed that fell to me as the wife.

"Will we need another suitcase for Porter?"

"There's one at the bottom of the closet, under his coats. Here, let me help you."

I sighed as she bustled around, but took mental notes. Next time, I would've preferred to complete the task myself.

Porter came in and took the suitcases without any effort. "I'm ready when you are." He smiled at me and winked.

A shiver willowed through my veins at that wink. Some things I hoped to never get used to.

We trotted along the dusty road in an open carriage which afforded us no protection from the weather or the dust — or the other people we would soon run into.

"I need to address what Adele brought up. I don't want to see any doubt of my character in your eyes."

I turned to him in a swift tick. "Do you see doubt in my eyes?"

"No. I don't. And I don't want a whisper to turn into that. That's why I want to tell you."

Benjamin neighed in agreement and so did I.

"Your sister is referring to one of two places. The first, I've alluded to. I was in the The Plots the night I heard your father trying to-sell you off." He stuttered it out. It still bothered him twice as much as it bothered me. "That night, I was collecting payment. If I don't go and collect the payments once a month, then I don't get paid. The owners aren't the most upstanding of citizens."

Disgust curled around my gut. "You loaned money to those people? What they do to women…"

"I wasn't the one who made the deal, Delilah. My father signed some less than upstanding mortgages. I'm trying to get out of them, but it seems no one wants to deal with those people. They were probably desperate when they approached my father about them in the first place."

I'd once heard Adele comfort Elaine when she thought her husband was visiting The Plots. She'd said that 'Boys will be boys.'

I never wanted to meet one of those boys.

Porter wasn't one of those kind.

"Why would Adele be there?"

He shrugged. "Maybe it wasn't her that saw me there. Maybe she's just repeating gossip."

Looking out across the swampy grass, I squinted against the sunlight, determined to heat me up despite the constant chill in my bones. Porter's word-of-mouth indiscretion was the last thing on my mind.

They would laugh—or worse, whisper. Whispering was the cruelest of offenses. Whispers held enough evil to rattle the strongest of hearts but not enough to be deemed a sin.

They would chastise him for his choice of bride.

"Where'd you go?"

His voice jolted me out of my self-loathing. "I'm here."

"I'm sorry. I will get out of any business with that side of town as soon as possible. I knew it would bother you. I'd planned to get rid of it all before you found out. I hate that place even more now."

"It's not that. Are you sure I should be going with you? It's not too early to turn around—or I could walk back."

With one jerk on the reins, he brought us to a complete halt. "Tell me the truth. You don't want to go with me?"

"I don't want to be an embarrassment to you."

He cracked a sideways smile and the reins on Benjamin's back. "You're the only one who still sees that scar, Delilah. I'm proud to have you as my wife."

That shut me up for the rest of the trip.

The city was concrete—all of it. The buildings were, for the most part, the same color and they matched the street, creating a singular wave of vision from the building to my own toes, never breaking pace.

It was ugly.

Yet beautiful in its bustling people. They gave the place color. Pink and peach colored dresses pockmarked the rest of the crowds of blue and gray ones, every woman done up as though they were prepped for a wedding—or a church service.

I'd never seen such fashion.

It looked painful.

Waists were cinched below hats that mimicked tiny top hats with bursts of flowers or colors to prove they were feminine.

I looked down at my drab burgundy dress and was thoroughly unimpressed either way.

There was no point in dressing up a ghastly beast.

"The hotel is over there where I usually stay. If you like it here, I was thinking about buying an apartment. The top floors of the hotel we are staying at are apartments." Seeing the quizzical look on my face, he chuckled. "We'll talk about that later."

My eyes flared at some things I'd never heard of but dared not ask about.

"Where else did you go?"

He knew exactly what I meant.

"I can show you tonight. It doesn't open until late in the afternoon. Are you hungry? We can get something to eat before or after we check into the hotel."

I wasn't hungry at all.

"Hotel it is. After that, maybe I can show you where I work." He grabbed my hand with the suggestion. "They've all been asking about you. They claim I'm keeping you hidden away. Don't. Don't even think it Delilah Jeansonne."

Transparency was a great skill of mine—at least around Porter.

Minutes later, he stopped the horse at a place marked the carriage house and paid a man to take Benjamin, grumbling about him being taken better care of there than at home.

"The hotel is right next door. Come on."

He offered his arm, though he was loaded down with suitcases. I saw a couple in front of us, the man and woman walking arm in arm as a boy no older than twelve struggled behind them, carrying their things.

I hoped he was getting paid well, but knew better.

"My father always said we shouldn't get too comfortable in our money that we forget to work hard," Porter whispered down to me.

I nodded, my eyes still trained on the thin boy who could've been my male counterpart.

"Porter, it's been weeks. We were beginning to think your new bride had you detained."

He laughed but I didn't recognize the sound.

"She's here. Delilah, this is Henry. He's the owner of this hotel. Anything you need, he can arrange it."

"It's nice to meet you, Henry. Thank you for the offer."

Henry, much shorter than Porter and much heavier, took the suitcases from Porter and bid us follow him up several flights of stairs to a room with double doors.

"We have it from here, Henry. Thank you."

He didn't move as Henry walked away, instead choosing to stare me down.

"Stay here one second."

Porter jangled the keys in the lock and after only one trip brought all of the suitcases in, shutting the door behind him. When he came out, his arms were empty and he threw both doors open wide.

Before I knew it, I was in those arms.

"What are you doing?"

He kissed my non-scarred temple and wrangled me into a more secure hold. "We never got to do this. I'm trying to make things right here. It may not be our home, but it's a threshold nonetheless. Here's to a happy honeymoon, my love."

I stayed stunned until he laid me down on the bed, covering my body with his.

"This is how it should've been. Alone. Like this. No one to bother us."

His gray eyes ran so deep. He studied me, his face hovering above mine, the rest of him deliciously weighing me down.

"We have to make up for lost time."

"Starting now." He spoke those words against my lips, the warmth sending spirals of bliss around every muscle in my body.

Hours later, my stomach gurgled. I hadn't heard that sound since marrying Porter.

"There I go, neglecting you again. Let's go eat and then I can show you the other place I have gone."

I stopped him with my hand on his chest. "Porter, it's fine. I don't need to know. I trust you."

He didn't budge.

"I think I needed to hear that more than 'I love you'. I'm still taking you. I want you to see. Never do I want to see doubt in your eyes."

"Let me get dressed and then I'll go wherever you'd like me to. This place is a little overwhelming."

"It can be. That's why I choose to keep my house and travel. The city has its pulls—its secrets, just like everywhere else. The key is not to get sucked in. Before I had a reason to go home, I'd considered moving here."

Taking a quick look in the mirror, I regressed to plaiting my hair over *that* side of my face.

Porter's voice startled me. I startled at the slightest of noises lately. "Trust me. It would hurt if you got any more beautiful. Let's go."

The man was a liar.

We ate at a restaurant that doted on us even more than Eliza, if that was possible. Porter didn't meet my gaze once during the meal, but then again, I wasn't looking at him either. There was more fine things in that one room than I'd seen in my life.

The women in the room gawked at me. There was plenty to look at. Besides my face, there was the obvious difference in my dress. Theirs was much the same, but a little tighter, a little more revealing.

"We can go to the other place now."

"Sure."

Porter paid for the meal with a flick of his wrist. He must've had a tab there. They knew him by name and didn't seem surprised to see his new wife seated across from him.

Again, he took my arm as we walked the streets. Other than a few gazes at my dress, I didn't get very much attention.

"It's through here."

Porter pointed lazily down a bricked hallway between two buildings. At the end was a tiny shack that resembled the cabin at the edge of Porter's property. As we approached, I saw flowers and plants that, from a distance, seemed to be dead, but bloomed the closer we got.

"What is this place?"

"Trust me."

"Who is here?"

My curiosity overrode my trust.

"This is the other place that I went—someplace they might've seen me. Someone might've seen me here."

He was still hung up on my stupid sister's gossip.

We entered the place, stepping over a line of salt around the threshold. A haunting wind chime moaned our arrival.

"I told you not to come ba..." The woman, dressed in the most colorful outfit I'd ever seen stuttered at my presence. "I see you've brought your destiny."

"My destiny?"

The dark-skinned woman hummed as she took her place in a chair that took up most of the room.

"I told that girl that she wasn't her destiny. Wasn't any use in trying to push against a wall."

Porter stepped forward, acknowledging her.

"Told who? Marie?"

"Marie? Is that what she's calling herself these days?"

I tugged on Porter's hand when he didn't immediately respond.

"I don't understand."

"Marie is not the name she was given. At least this time she picked a good French name. Shame she ended the cycle."

"When I came here before, you wouldn't tell me anything about her. Why now?"

The woman rolled her eyes and fiddled with an alligator head, one of two that made up the arms of her chair. "Couldn't talk about it until she was gone. Well, until she expired."

Porter's jaw ground against itself while his face reddened.

"But she's not—gone—she's still here—tormenting us."

"You can't just kill the vessel. You must cut the tether. Don't be ridiculous. Your mama knew how these things went."

Porter attempted to lunge at the woman, but was frozen by something invisible.

"Now, now, Jeansonne. Nothing worthwhile was ever achieved by force. Come here, child. Your husband is going to take a minute to recover." Beside me, Porter's face has turned ashen, his eyes were fixed straight ahead like he'd been seized in time never to recover.

Her bangle covered wrist lifted as her hand reached out for me. Her skin was silken, it reminded me of the fabric Adele's dress had been made of.

Turning my hand over and over again, she studies the lines with the tip of her index finger. The place is quiet. I expect a dramatic entrance any minute by someone needing a hex or worse.

"She grows, doesn't she? First appearing to you as a little cher and now growing every time you see her. Why do you suppose that is?"

The ludicrous answer knocked at the back of my mind, but I knew better than to make myself look like a fool. "You had to fall in love with him, didn't you? That's where all the trouble began. The more you fell in love, the older she got. The older she got, the more cracks in her contract."

"Contract?"

"Mmm…there's no such thing as a one way deal in this house."

Instead of answering anything, the tiny woman with the royal disposition was only posing more questions.

"Ever see a picture of Porter's grandmother?"

I shook my head. We hadn't gotten that far.

"She looks an awful lot like Marie, mais non?"

"I don't know."

"Well, did you know that a spirit can revive itself, generation after generation? Come back and cause all kinds of hell to the ones they despise? Of course, it requires a great deal of know how."

I shook my head against the nonsensical rattling of information. The way she held my hand made my head foggy and my thoughts dim.

"His mother, that fat tub, made the same choice as you. Falling in love with one of the Jeansonne's didn't fall into Marie's plan. Come to think of it, neither did her lover murdering her. Either way, she's gone."

"She's not gone. She haunts us." Porter's tone grew desperate for more information as did my heart.

"That's because she's only half of the deal. The bastard must die too. I can…" She canted her head to the side, regarding us with a sinister half-grin. "Take care of the situation for you."

My brain screamed against the idea.

"At what cost? If I've learned anything in this life, it's that nothing is free."

At the boom of his voice, she released my hand and latched onto Porter's. Again, he was stilled in place.

"Your money is worth nothing except kindling in my house."

"If not money, what?"

"A future favor. I name the price at a later date. Could be next year. Could be the next lifetime. But your friend would be gone and this time for good."

I took a few steps back from the confrontation and the potentially life-altering deal on the table. The links this woman had planted were finally starting to form a chain. Everything was connected.

And Porter had circumvented a grave mistake.

My eyes broadened with the realization.

"Are you saying that Marie is the reincarnatioMarin of Porter's grandmother?"

A wind of disgust blew through the dishrag curtained windows.

"I doubt she would've ever consummated the marriage. Anyway, his grandmother, the one he knew, was his step-grandmother. They weren't actually related. Collette killed his real grandmother. Oh...poor Porter. Doesn't even know his true family history."

Insincerity poured from her mouth like melted wax. This whole twisted scheme was her doing, along with her cohorts, and she took pride in the mess she'd made and the rubble in its wake.

She let go of his hand and wiped her own back and forth as though wiping the dirt from her hands—along with any subsiding guilt.

"And my mother?"

"Your mother, like this chit, wasn't part of the plan. Marie was to marry you, the house and all your wealth would be hers and then she and Rebel would murder you. I suspect that Marie grew a conscious after three generations of lying and deceit and killed herself over it. She's stupider than you. Half of your wealth was my cut. And now it's gone."

Her lament over the lost money was the most genuine emotion she'd expressed so far.

"Do whatever it takes. Get rid of her."

"And the boy?"

"I'll break my grandfather's contract. Wait…that was part of it too. To keep Rebel close to us."

"Ahhh…the story is still unfolding."

Spiders crawled along my arms and webs clouded my vision.

"We need to leave, Porter. Now."

There was no time to wait for his answer. Pulling him by his jacket, I trudged through the room at a slow pace, feeling like the door grew further and further from my reach with every step.

"Help me, husband."

At the word, his attention snapped to me and broke the sludge we were buried in. We reached the door and at the touch of dusk's sleepy sunlight on our faces, we were free from the grasp of evil that clutched the air of that shack and its mistress.

Except now we were strapped into a deal with the core of our repression.

"What will she ask of us?" I whispered as we walked numb into the falling night.

"Me. She will ask something of me. This has nothing to do with you. Let's get you back to the hotel before more demons find us."

His tone stung. Even in the precipice of our ghosts, he'd always said we would get through it together.

My heart cracked. I was alone again.

Chapter Twenty

Porter

Processing the compilation of lies would be no small task, but it was secondary to Delilah. I should've never gone to The Plots that night. I should've sent someone to collect my debt.

Paying a price for Delilah was the biggest mistake I'd ever made.

She'd probably be married off to someone normal by now if I hadn't felt the compulsion to have her for myself.

Even being alone would be infinitely better than being married to an impetuous bastard who can't even decipher the lies right under his nose.

"Why are we running?"

Her voice, as it always had, stopped my haste. "I'm sorry. I just want you as far away from all of that as soon as possible."

"I'm not scared, Porter. I know you will keep me safe. You always have."

The truth in those tomorrow eyes killed me. She believed her own words, no matter how far from the truth they were. I would always *attempt* to protect her from the world. My ability to do so was the subject in question.

"I've done a pathetic job of it. But that ends tonight."

She caught me in a dead stare, attempting to get a reaction from me. She would get none, mostly because I couldn't look her in the eyes again. That clear blue unabashed love staring back at me clung to my heart and would never allow me to follow through with what I needed to do.

What I should've done in the first place.

"What are you talking about?"

"I'm leaving tomorrow morning after I go to the bank."

I stuffed clothing into my suitcase without a care.

"Where are you going?"

"Home."

The bed slumped with her light weight as she sat on the side.

"Maybe I should ask where I'm going. Isn't that what's happening? You've decided this is all too much? I'm not worth the money after all, right? To think, we almost made it a month."

"That's not what I think at all. I think I should've set you free before you were involved in all of this. This is not worth it. I'm not worth it."

She stalked across the room and every cell in me came to life. All I wanted to do was for her to tell me it was worth it. That she loved me. That she was happy. That I'd given her something she would've never been able to have with her parents.

It was then, looking down into her blue eyes that a surge of strength took hold of me. It was the same swell that originally seeded the first time I saw her. I knew that day, that I could take her out of the shadows.

I knew the minute her petite foot touched the ground at the base of the stairs that I could show her light when all she did was hide in the darkness.

Except all I'd done was rob one darkness to replace it by another.

She put her delicate hands on either side of my face. Her skin had always been soft, despite the hard labor which had taken up most of her adolescence.

My eyes drew downward, not able to face her.

"Look at me, Porter. If you've never looked at me before, look at me now."

"I've always seen you, Delilah."

"So you know that when I speak, I only speak the truth."

"Tell me your truth. Tell me it one last time."

The sting of pain caused me to hold my breath before the full weight of her act piqued my mind. She'd slapped me.

"I'm sorry." Her hands covered her mouth. "Don't you dare leave me, Porter Jeansonne. Don't even think about it."

My heart beat in my chest. It sounded like Benjamin's galloping hoofs between my temples.

"All I wanted was for you to have a better life."

"And I do. Even in the simplest of definitions, Porter. I do."

"We've just made a deal with someone who doesn't forget things, Delilah. She could ask for anything in return. Don't you understand that?"

With hands on her hips, she looked to the heavens. Closing her eyes she sent a prayer to heaven. I couldn't hear all of the words, but saw when she muttered 'help me'.

"Whatever she asks of us, we will provide. We can't worry about a future that hasn't come. We can only hope for the best. If I learned nothing else from my wretched childhood, it was that."

I sank to the chair behind me in a slump. I'd never wanted her exposed to anything but happiness.

"How did this happen?" I darted my eyes around the room, asking the furniture as much as anyone else. "I went to save you and here you are saving me. I think you've been saving me from the beginning. I couldn't live without you if I wanted to. I want you in my arms in the mornings and I want your laughter at my table. I just—I didn't know what else to do. Forgive me, love."

I waited for her response. Instead of speaking, she crossed the room and sat in my lap, burying her face between my neck and my shoulder, her fists holding onto me for dear life.

I loved this woman in my arms.

I'd been empty and cold before her.

We stayed like that for hours. Her warm breaths filtered through my shirt, warming me and my heart over and over like the most reliable of clocks.

Early the next morning, I woke before Delilah. Though I'd come into town for business, all I wanted to do was remove my wife far away from this grime-filled place. The city had lost its luster next to her.

Before leaving, we stopped in at my office and I handled the immediate business and left as soon as I could.

The only thing I wanted was to get home with Delilah.

"Are you sure there's not more you want to do?" She asked after we'd already left the outskirts of the city.

"I'm sure. I think I'm going to work from home from now on. If they need things signed or a meeting in person, they will have to come to me."

She stared at me for a while before speaking. "I thought the city had its hooks in you."

"That was before you got your hooks in me."

The entire way home, we avoided the bigger issue. I didn't want to scare her any more than she had been.

"It's going to be quiet without Marie around. She's been with me for so long. It will be like mourning her again."

Delilah straightened her skirt and dusted off some invisible dirt from her shoes. "I'm sure we could find things to do."

Her blush told me the full intentions of her meaning.

"I'm sure we can."

"Can I ask you something?"

"Always."

"I'm still trying to wrap my head around everything and I'm sure there's more to discover. But why? Why would someone go to all that trouble? Just for your money?"

"Once, when I was small, I overheard my mother tell someone—it must've been June or maybe another maid—that above all, every woman wants to be young and beautiful and every man wants to be rich. I've always thought it was complete insanity, but in Marie's case, I think maybe she was right. All this time they were after my family's money. I know she was always asking me if she was pretty and complained when I didn't tell her that enough. Maybe we'll never know the depth of their deceit. Maybe it's better if we don't know.

"I guess that's why she hated me. You didn't love her because she was ugly on the inside and you love me even though I'm..."

"I love you because you are beautiful in every way possible."

We rode for a few more hours before she spoke again.

"I stole the necklace from Rebel. It was hanging in the stables."

"And what if you had gotten caught? I would've killed him if he hurt you."

She looked ahead, to the road that led us home with her chin up. There were so few times that she faced forward with her chin jutted out in strength that I made sure to pay attention to the next words from her mouth.

Inherently, I knew they would be important.

"I didn't think about myself. I only thought if I could get the necklace that somehow it would rid me of the ghost—and in doing away with the ghost—you could not be so—haunted." She paused. "You know Rebel killed Marie, don't you? I know we haven't accused him out loud, but there's no doubt in my mind."

"I do. I had no idea that I'd married an investigator. Honestly, I am a fool for not thinking of it myself. They were involved. Everyone knew it."

"You can't very well figure things out if you're wallowing in unfounded guilt."

For the rest of the afternoon, I listened to the sounds of Delilah through the house. No longer was my house silent. The issues that surrounded us weren't buried, but merely creeping below the surface, awaiting their turn to be resurrected.

I feared the repayment to the woman I'd traded for peace.

I anticipated resistance on Rebel's behalf in ending the contract, but I hoped that a little added blackmail on my part would curtail his efforts.

But most of all, I feared Delilah's happiness.

Would she ever be able to forgive me for everything I'd put her through?

"He's out there again, Porter." My mother poked her head into my office, but kept her feet on the other side of its threshold.

I growled and she grabbed her chest. "I'm sorry, Mother."

"It's fine. He makes me jumpy. For the last few days he's been looking for something all over the grounds. In the bushes, in the back near the pond. It's disconcerting to say the least. June tried to run him away from the porch yesterday with the broom, but he came back minutes later. He's frantic with whatever he's lost."

"I'll take care of it. He won't be working here any longer."

"It's about time. He's a creepy little man."

My mother called every man little.

After she left, I got up from my desk at the sound of commotion outside. Rebel was talking to Delilah from afar, but her posture and clenched fists told me exactly how his presence was making her feel.

Rushing outside, I vowed to interrupt his presence.

"Rebel, you need to leave." Shouting the command, I hoped to get his attention off of her and onto me. I stepped in front of Delilah but she refused to be in my shadow.

My wife was done cowering.

"I work here."

"You're not working. Slinking around looking in plants and in the dirt is not working. You don't know the meaning of work." Delilah interjected before I could form the words.

"I've lost something. I have to find it."

It was with the scratch of his voice that I initially noticed Rebel's appearance. While he'd never been well put together, he resembled a roughed-up savage. Deep circles cradled his eyes and even with our distance I could see the clods of dirt underneath his fingernails.

"I said leave!"

He ignored my second demand and I took one step toward him, determined to back my words up with a solid promise.

"Rebel, you would've found it by now. Don't you think it would've shone in the sunlight?"

My chest seized with her question. Rebel was operating under the premise that we had no idea what he hunted for.

She'd blown that theory away with the most innocent of intentions.

"Who said it was shiny?" His tone singed my ears with hostility.

"No one. I just—assumed—it was something precious— why else would you be searching so—I…"

"It was you! I thought you were just in the stables looking for a little side action. You were stealing from me."

"She found it. I told her to keep it. It is my property after all."

I shook with the lies that so easily flowed from my mouth.

"Found it? And where is it now? It's mine!"

"Why do you need it? Tell us why it's so important and maybe we will consider giving it back."

Delilah stood true. Not even a flinch touched her body at my blatant dig for information.

"It was Marie's. I loved her. It's the only thing I have left of her."

"You loved her so much you killed her."

There was no bounce back time from my statement. I thought it would surprise him that I knew.

"At least while she was alive and—not acting stupid—I didn't treat her like dirt."

"I was honest with her about my feelings. It was an arranged marriage."

He huffed out a laugh through his nose. "Is that what you thought? An arranged marriage."

"Wasn't it?"

My trouble was that I constantly craved answers to questions that should've died with Marie.

"It was arranged by us, if that's what you mean," he sneered.

"No. That's not what I meant. I don't even care. Just leave us alone. There's nothing for you here. Marie is gone. There's no reason for you to still be around."

He snorted. "Marie is not gone. She won't be gone until I release her."

"She's been released. I haven't seen her. You haven't seen her. She's gone. You should've let her go in peace years ago."

He nearly snapped his neck, Delilah his target. "He needed to suffer like I have."

"It's over, Rebel. She's gone. The necklace is destroyed. There's nothing for you here."

"She doesn't forget her debts, you know. I bet you think you're safe now—just like I did."

"Let's go, Delilah."

I turned to go back into the house, extending my hand for Delilah to follow me.

He'd moved so fast, I didn't have time to stop him.

As I turned a roar broke free from my throat.

His hands were curled around Delilah's neck. As I reached out he squeezed, making her squirm.

He had my whole life in his grip.

"Don't."

"Or what?"

"I'll kill you. I swear it."

"No one has to die. Just give me what I want—what I've wanted all along."

I'd give him everything if he'd just let her go. Delilah's knees faltered, bending under the loss of blood to her brain.

"Anything. Anything you want."

"No, Porter." She pulled a mutinous breath through her nose and her eyes rolled back in her head.

"I said anything, you bastard!"

"I want it all."

"It's yours. I'll sign the papers today."

"Do it now."

I shoved my hands out toward him. The sheer anger made my voice quiver. "At least let her breathe."

With a tick of his head, he looked at Delilah as though he'd forgotten that he was draining her of life by the second. Releasing her neck, he grabbed a fistful of hair and pushed her in the direction of the house.

I thanked God my mother and June had left the house though I could still hear their voices in the front. I hoped they stayed there. I was afraid of what Rebel might do with more witnesses.

"Here." I scribbled a pathetic statement about giving all of my money to Rebel that would never hold up in court. But he didn't know that. I thrust it in his direction and watched as he read, little by little letting go of Delilah's hair. Her eyes and mine stayed locked, but out of the corner of my eye, I saw her hand move—just a little.

I shook my head, telling and begging her to just go along with me.

I should've known better.

In a move that rivaled Rebel's earlier swiftness, she slid my silver letter opener from my desk and flicked it around in her hand, the pointed side facing him.

He never let go of the paper long enough to see what fate awaited him.

He was too interested in the contract that would never come to fruition.

The blade, no sharper than a butter knife, knew its duty, flawlessly slitting into Rebel's gut.

Delilah ran around the desk, launching herself into my arms with a cry.

"She…" Rebel began, now inspecting the damage.

We were too far away from town to do anything about it — even if I wanted to save him.

He deserved his fate.

And I finally received mine.

Epilogue

Delilah

Six Years Later

With one finger underneath the circle of pearls around my child's wrist, I reveled in the sight of her father's dimple at the side of her chin.

My other daughter had the same dimple.

I saw it once before she was taken from me.

Porter is enamored with Brynna, just as I had been with Katie. In secret, I'd given her my middle name of Catherine, but then changed it to Katie, because like her life, it was short yet sweet.

One child can never replace the other in a mother's heart. A piece of my soul will always be in the possession of that pint-sized voodoo woman. Her payment was great.

My heart thumps against the remembrance. Katie's heart beat seven times before another image in the corner took my attention on the day of her birth, with blood still clotting against her fragile skin, the woman in the corner reached out and took her payment in full.

"What are you thinking about?" Porter asks me, placing a gentle kiss to my temple.

I thank the heavens he wasn't allowed into the room with me when Katie was born—he would've tried to put a stop to acts which could never be reversed.

Before she shifted into silent smoke, the woman held my ghostly child in her arms as though she'd just emerged from *her* womb instead of mine.

"She's got your dimple." I respond, not really lying, but not disclosing the full truth either. Hiding Katie's death from him has been the greatest sacrifice. To the midwives that surrounded me, Katie's death was a complication from the stress of birth. At least, that's what they called it.

Porter was under the same assumption and I allowed him to stay that way.

His haunted heart was free.

And my haunting had just begun.

"That she does. But her eyes, those twilight blues, are straight from her mother."

"You can't pass down scars."

He grunted—a noise that I associated with his disapproval.

A knock at the door gave me an out for what would surely be an hour-long discussion about how beautiful I was—I would agree just to end it.

He flung the door open and June whispered something about dinner. We'd been taking our meals when we could, around Brynna's schedule and Eliza spoke to us several times—more like whined in a loving way about our absence.

"Tell Mother we will be down soon."

I spoke to my daughter in hushed tones, telling her that her grandmother was jealous and wanting more time with her—which was the truth. Porter and I were downright selfish with our new family member—especially me.

"Her admirers await." He whispered in my ear, causing a slew of goosebumps to break out over my skin. From this vantage point, Marie's grave could be seen in the distance. We'd given her a new headstone, closer to the house. Porter thought it was creepy, but she served as a reminder that even the hardest of hearts can come around.

As far as Rebel—Porter and I had only spoken of him once—shortly after I stabbed him. The words were never explicitly spoken, but that night, the alligators in Bayou Sorrel got a hefty supper.

No one ever asked about him or his whereabouts.

There were questions that would remain unanswered. I'd become content with not knowing. Marie had her reasons for deciding that enough was enough in her and Rebel's charade. We'd never know why Rebel allowed his greed to make such a convoluted deal with a woman whose power kept them in her clutches.

The secrets of this place were as deep as the swamp.

Somehow, I preferred them that way.

Brynna kicked in my arms, bringing me back to the present. I thought about letting her go for a few minutes and didn't appreciate the notion. A simple sigh was my response.

"I was thinking maybe we could take a night off tonight — maybe go to the cabin."

"That would be nice. But she's still so little."

He laughed. "She's almost six months old and you haven't left her side. What are you worried about?"

"Nothing." I answered, turning my face away from him.

"I told you. There's no sign of her. I've had people on the lookout."

On one of his trips to the city, Porter noticed that everything about that woman, the one who held our fate in her hands, had vanished.

Of course she had vanished. She had collected her steep debt.

"I know. What if something happens and we're too far away?"

"My mother raised me and I turned out fine."

A raised eyebrow gave away my inner sarcasm.

"Oh, I saw that! Well, at least your sense of humor is intact. Come on, let's not smother the beauty. Anyway, I kind of want you to myself for a change."

"How can I deny that?"

He took our daughter in his hands, leaving me cold from her absence.

"Let's go. We'll decide what to do later."

As he gazed down into our baby girl's eyes with one hand cradling her head and the other balancing her bottom in his hands I could see who he was had shifted since I'd come into his life.

Once I thought I couldn't bring anything to him but shame and pain.

Once he thought his life would lead nowhere.

He was the cure for my steadfast loneliness and search for belonging.

And I was the cure for his haunted heart.

Other Works
by
Lila Felix

THE LOVE AND SKATE SERIES:
LOVE AND SKATE
HOW IT ROLLS
DOWN N DERBY
CAUGHT IN A JAM
FALSE START

THE SECOND JAM (A LOVE AND SKATE SPIN-OFF NOVEL)

BAYOU BEAR CHRONICLES:
BURDEN
HEARTEN
ENGRAVEN (SPRING 2015)

FORCED AUTONOMY (A DYSTOPIAN NOVELLA SERIAL)

UNTIL SHE WALKED IN
HEARTBREAKER
DETHRONING CROWN
SEEKING HAVOK
EMERGE
PERCHANCE
HOAX

Lila Felix

LILA'S ANTICS:

WWW.LILAFELIX.COM
WWW.AUTHORLILAFELIX.BLOGSPOT.COM

WWW.FACEBOOK.COM/AUTHORLILAFELIX
TWITTER: @AUTHORLILAFELIX
EMAIL: AUTHORLILAFELIX@GMAIL.COM

Acknowledgements:

To Mr. Felix: I hope you always haunt my heart. These trials we are going through will one day be over and the hospital will be a faint memory.

To the Rink Rats: I wish you could see the smile that comes to my face when I think about the love and support you all show me. I'm overwhelmed.

To Anne Eliot: Thanks for opening my eyes, no matter how many toothpicks it takes.

Ashleigh Russell: Your friendship never fails.

Felicia Tatum: My new friend, I am so blessed to have you.

272